Faith-Filled Fiction™

www.faith-filledfiction.com | www.vikkikestell.com

LAYNIE PORTLAND, SPY RISING—THE PREQUEL

Laynie Portland | Book 1
Vikki Kestell
Also Available in eBook Format

BOOKS BY VIKKI KESTELL

LAYNIE PORTLAND

Book 1: *Laynie Portland, Spy Rising—The Prequel*
Book 2: *Laynie Portland, Retired Spy*
Book 3: *Laynie Portland, Renegade Spy*
Book 4: *Laynie Portland, Spy Resurrected*

NANOSTEALTH

Book 1: *Stealthy Steps*
Book 2: *Stealth Power*
Book 3: *Stealth Retribution*
Book 4: *Deep State Stealth* (2019 Selah Award Winner)

A PRAIRIE HERITAGE

Book 1: *A Rose Blooms Twice*
Book 2: *Wild Heart on the Prairie*
Book 3: *Joy on This Mountain*
Book 4: *The Captive Within*
Book 5: *Stolen*
Book 6: *Lost Are Found*
Book 7: *All God's Promises*
Book 8: *The Heart of Joy—A Short Story* (eBook only)

GIRLS FROM THE MOUNTAIN

Book 1: *Tabitha*
Book 2: *Tory*
Book 3: *Sarah Redeemed*

LAYNIE PORTLAND, SPY RISING—THE PREQUEL

ISBN-13: 978-1-970120-19-6
ISBN-10: 1-970120-19-3

LAYNIE PORTLAND, SPY RISING—THE PREQUEL

Laynie Portland | Book 1

Vikki Kestell

Also Available in eBook Format

LP

NO ONE IS BORN A SPY.

In one way or another, every "righteous" clandestine operative is sought out, enlisted, and trained for the difficult and often terrible work intended to ensure that the principles of freedom triumph over ideologies that seek to dominate and enslave.

The year is 1977; the Cold War is intensifying. Helena Portland—Laynie to her family—is set to graduate from the University of Washington, when recruiters from Marstead International invite her to dinner and an informal employment interview. Laynie is flattered: Marstead International is a technology and aeronautics firm with a global presence and reputation.

But behind their corporate image? Marstead is a front for joint U.S./NATO covert operations.

Not far into the dinner conversation, the recruiters make their pitch: "We have offices around the world, Miss Portland, and we actively seek college graduates with the right mix of aptitude and skills to work and grow within our worldwide market. Actually, we have been observing you for some time. We feel that you have the potential to serve . . . the interests of your country."

Laynie catches their drift and confronts it. "Let me see if I understand you correctly. You are representatives of a U.S. intelligence agency, unnamed so far, and you are trying to recruit me. Do I have it right?"

When Laynie accepts Marstead's offer, she is sent through the Company's rigorous tradecraft and tactical training program. Laynie soon discovers that the world of clandestine service is dirty business. To succeed, operatives must bend and twist the tenets of liberty. Along the way, noble objectives tarnish and corrode, hearts harden, and methods and means drag virtue into the gutter.

Laynie perseveres at the work set before her; she enters into it because she holds a secret—a secret she has never shared with anyone, a view of herself that not only condones the awful choices she is asked to make, but justifies them: *I am worthless; my life has no value. I am only useful when the work I do serves a greater purpose.*

ACKNOWLEDGEMENTS

LP

ALL MY THANKS AND APPRECIATION
to my esteemed teammates,
Cheryl Adkins and **Greg McCann.**
With every project, you give of yourselves,
pouring invaluable time from your busy lives
into each new book,
to make it the most effective instrument
of the Good News possible.
I love and appreciate you.
I always will.

MANY THANKS TO MY FRIEND,
Jim Rutskie,
for your technical expertise on firearms
and your enthusiasm for my books!
You are so appreciated.

SCRIPTURE QUOTATIONS

THE KING JAMES VERSION (KJV),
Public Domain.

COVER DESIGN

Vikki Kestell

FOREWORD

WHAT IS A PREQUEL? It is the inverse of a sequel; it is a book occurring *before* the actual first work in a series, whereas a sequel is the book that follows the first work and continues the story. A prequel serves as "the backstory," providing the reader with intimate, inside information concerning the series' protagonist.

Laynie Portland, Spy Rising—The Prequel, while being the first book in a four-book series, is, likewise, a look back into young Laynie's life, how Marstead International recruited her . . . and how they molded Laynie into the spy and seductress they desired her to be.

This statement is true: *No one is born a spy*. Laynie's journey into a life of counterintelligence and espionage required intense training and dedication, but that journey is also a tale of choices, of decisions often made for the wrong reasons and on the basis of faulty belief and rationale. Laynie's story discloses the inexorable breaking down of moral restraint as the pressure of *what she desires* overrules *what she knows is right* . . . when the innocence of her youth is stripped away, and the shape of her destiny is set.

Many of us will relate.

Laynie Portland
SPY RISING

PART 1: LAYNIE

LP

CHAPTER 1

LP

SEATTLE, WASHINGTON, MAY 1977

"HEY, MAMA."

Laynie's mother, Polly, stood at the kitchen sink, scrubbing vegetables for a chopped salad. Laynie sidled up to her mother, wrapped her arms around Polly's shoulders, and leaned down to press a kiss to her cheek.

Laynie's athletic frame towered a good eight inches over Polly Portland, who barely topped five feet and whose corkscrew ebony curls were distinctly unlike Laynie's straight blonde hair. Polly's husband, Gene Portland, was tall and lanky like Laynie. Although his blonde hair had darkened, then silvered, as he aged, most observers assumed Laynie had inherited her height and coloring from him.

She hadn't.

"Hey yourself, baby girl. How was your day?"

"All right. Last term paper of the semester turned in. *Check!* Two more finals, a group presentation, and I'm done."

"Your daddy and I are so proud of you, Laynie. First girl in the family on either side to earn hersel' a college degree."

"You keep saying that, but you and daddy gave me this opportunity, Mama. You worked and saved all my life to pay my way. I just stood on your shoulders; you and daddy 'earned' this degree."

"We wanted to give you every 'vantage we never had, sugar. Wouldn't have it no other way, and we know you will do us proud. By the way, got you a letter, came t'day."

"Probably another university hawking their graduate program. Well, I don't want to go to grad school. I want to get out in the world. Do some real work. See some things."

Laynie's parents had hinted that she should pursue a master's degree, but she'd roundly rebuffed the idea, and they hadn't pressed it further.

"Throw it away then, Laynie-girl. It's on the table."

"Okay. Thanks, Mama."

Laynie picked up the envelope, surprised not to see a university crest in the return address corner. The paper was expensive, a stiff powder blue with only an embossed P.O box to hint at the sender. She used her father's letter opener to slit the envelope, then pulled out a single sheet of folded stationery. Same stiff powder blue with a letterhead that read:

MARSTEAD INTERNATIONAL
Global Technologies of the Future

"Oh?" Laynie's pulse quickened, and she read through the letter quickly.

Dear Miss Portland,

Our company, Marstead International, is in the Seattle area interviewing prospective employees for entry-level positions in the field of technology acquisition and transfer. We understand that you will be graduating next month from the University of Washington. Marstead has offices throughout the world, and your degree in political science with a minor in modern languages suggests you would make a promising candidate.

If you are interested in hearing more about opportunities with Marstead, our recruitment team would like to host you for dinner at Metropolitan Grill, Second and Marion, downtown Seattle, Tuesday evening, 6 p.m., for an informal discussion and first interview. Please call us at the number below to confirm your reservation with us.

Cordially,
Regina Lohwen
Marstead International,
Human Resources Division

The letter piqued Laynie's curiosity. She picked up the phone and made the call. When she finished, she returned to the kitchen and collected flatware and plates to set the table.

"Guess what, Mama? I have my first job interview."

THE FOLLOWING TUESDAY evening, Laynie walked into the restaurant lobby. A man and a woman stood to greet her.

"Miss Portland? I'm Bert Norwood of Marstead International. This is my colleague, Angela Stewart."

Laynie nodded and shook hands with the man and woman, both "seasoned" personnel—in other words, a couple decades older and more experienced than her twenty-two years.

"Please call me Laynie."

"All right, Laynie, and feel free to call us Angela and Bert. If you'd like to come this way? I'm told our table is ready."

Laynie followed them through the restaurant and sat down at a table for three set in a corner that offered them privacy for their conversation.

After they had ordered from the menu, Bert asked, "Why don't you tell us what you'd like to do with your life, Laynie?"

A curious approach, Laynie thought. *Most companies want to know what you can offer them. They want you to speak to why they should hire you—or at least that's what I've been told to expect.* Laynie had taken a workshop in interviewing techniques, part of which was preparing to present herself in a favorable light, to demonstrate how she might be an asset to the company.

She smiled. "Thank you for asking. Well, I suppose at the deepest level, I'd like my work to harmonize with my personal values and goals. I want my life's labor to count for something positive. Meaningful. The technology field is growing quickly, and I feel that it will, within the next few decades, impact all aspects of the human experience. I'd like to contribute to that, to making the world a better place."

Her response must have been received favorably, because Bert replied, "Marstead, too, holds corporate values focused on improving lives through technology. It is actually very important to us that our employees share our desire to make the world a better, safer, and freer place for all people."

Laynie maintained a neutral expression as she repeated his last words to herself, *Safer? Freer? Hmm. Interesting shift to the dialogue.*

Bert continued, "We have offices around the world, Miss Portland, and we actively seek college graduates with the right mix of aptitude and skills to work and grow within our worldwide market. Are you averse to travel? Perhaps relocating to one of our international offices?"

"Not at all. I'd like to see more of the world."

"I'm glad to hear it. A willingness to travel and relocate advances your candidacy with Marstead. In addition, we look for people who can become comfortable in diverse cultures and environments, able to successfully navigate within them. To that end, we offer our new employees rigorous training, such as immersive language instruction and technology adoption and coaching to make them proficient in their specific positions. We also pay tuition for employees wishing to pursue graduate degrees while in our employ."

Laynie nodded. "I like the sound of that."

"Laynie, is your family, by chance, of Scandinavian descent? I ask because you have classic Scandinavian features—the height, blonde hair, and blue eyes."

"My father's family is Swedish, but I can't claim his heritage. I was adopted, you see. It was a closed adoption, so I know nothing of my biological parents' pedigree."

She laughed softly. "My dad has the Swedish characteristics, all right, but my mother is African American. She's a little thing, too. I was taller than her before I started junior high."

"You come from a loving family, I take it?" Angela asked.

"Very much so. There are just the four of us, my parents, me, and my younger brother, Sammie." She chuckled again. "Sorry. His name is actually Stephen, but I've called him Sammie my whole life."

"Do you have other family, Laynie? Aunts? Uncles? Grandparents? Cousins?"

"No, not that we are in contact with. I'm afraid my parents' families, on both sides, didn't approve of mixed marriages, so they severed ties. Like I said, just the four of us."

"How would your family feel if you relocated, say, to Europe?"

Laynie thought for a moment. "I think it would be hard for them to accept my choice."

"And you? How might their feelings affect you?"

She met Angela's probing gaze. "I would hope they understand that I must follow my dreams and aspirations. Although the distance might be difficult for them to bear, they have always supported my decisions—and it's not as though we'd never see each other again. The world is getting smaller by the minute."

The waiter appeared with their entrees, and they waited until he finished serving before resuming their conversation.

As they began to eat, Angela turned the conversation back to business. "To be frank, Laynie, we think you are the type of individual Marstead is looking for: bold, flexible, adaptive, smart. In fact, our Marstead Talent Acquisition Department has been observing you for some time."

"Oh?" Laynie was picking up an odd "vibe" from the two recruiters, but she determined to show no surprise at Angela's comment, even though she *was* surprised. Very. But then, she had always been good at masking her feelings.

Angela glanced at Bert as though seeking his confirmation for something. Bert nodded for her to continue.

Angela smiled. "Yes, as it turns out, you are high on our list of potential new hires. Not only is your academic record outstanding, but your gift for languages intrigues us. You are fluent in Spanish and German, I believe?"

"Spanish more than German, but, yes—and a smattering of Swedish, thanks to my dad."

"Good, good. Adaptability to new situations and facility with language is important in the technology acquisition work we do in foreign countries such as France, Norway, Finland, Estonia, Poland, Germany. And the Soviet Union.

Without skipping a beat, Angela added, "Have you any interest in learning Russian? Tech transfer is difficult enough without the addition of language barriers. We, of course, want to bring any emerging tech home to the States. We wish American industry to continue as the best in the world—while we also keep America strong and secure. How do those goals align with your personal values?"

An instinct humming in Laynie's head told her to play it cool, even, perhaps, *coy*.

What are they really asking me?

She said, "I would enjoy learning Russian," but her political science studies were chasing her thoughts down a different path. *Marstead acquires technology from the Soviet Union? Hmm. How do they do that? And I wonder how Leonid Brezhnev feels about it? Bet you a doughnut he's clueless about Marstead's plans to "bring home emerging tech," particularly Soviet tech, Angela—but you probably wouldn't take that bet, would you?*

Angela, still pleasant, still probing carefully, said next, "Based on what we've seen of you, we feel that you have the character, aptitude, and potential to serve . . . the interests of your country, Laynie."

There it was.

Laynie snapped to the sudden twist in the conversation—confirmation of what, moments earlier, she'd begun to suspect. Nonetheless, she didn't question the abrupt turn. She didn't even flick an eyebrow, but only glanced with indifference at the woman . . . who was watching Laynie a little too closely for her comfort.

This has got to be an interview for an altogether different kind of job, and I don't particularly appreciate being played with. I wonder how you'd like it, Bert and Angela?

Let's find out, shall we?

Laynie speared some green beans and sighed a happy sigh. "I just *love* how they've prepared these beans, don't you, Angela?"

Angela, taken aback at the alteration in Laynie's affect, blinked. "I, uh, yes. They're quite good."

She slid her eyes toward Bert. At Laynie's gushing pronouncement, he had forked a bite of the beans and, at present, was looking them over as if seeing green beans for the first time in his life. He popped the bite into his mouth, and chewed.

He met Angela's questioning look and shrugged. "Sure. They're okay."

"But they're cooked to perfection, don't you agree? Not overdone or underdone. It is *so* hard to achieve the right balance."

A young bus boy paused at their table to refill their water glasses.

Laynie looked up and smiled. Shifted a little toward him. Lifted her chin. "Hello there."

"Oh. Hi. Can I get you anything?"

Laynie dimpled, placed her elbow on the table and rested her chin on her palm. "I dunno. What are you offering?"

Color washed up the teen's neck. He stammered, "I-I . . . um, I-I." He glanced across the room. "I think m-my manager is waving at me." He hurried away.

Laynie giggled. "What a cutie. Do you think I embarrassed him? I did, didn't I?" Her giggle became a full-throated laugh. "Well, I'm sure he'll get over it. Me? I'm looking forward to dessert—I saw that they have lemon meringue pie on the menu. I just *love* lemon meringue pie, don't you?"

Bert—astounded into watchful silence, uncertain of what he was witnessing, but fascinated by it nonetheless—nodded.

"Well, I do hope the pie is *fresh*." Laynie leaned across the table and confided, "If lemon pie isn't fresh, the meringue—you know, the fluffy white part? It gets all chewy and gross."

Angela and Bert's chins descended and rose in silent, synchronous agreement, mesmerized by Laynie's performance.

Then Laynie set down her fork and sat back, her expression serene, but knowing. "So, you were saying about new employee training?"

Laynie yanked herself out of her memories and glanced up. "Except for the normal ups and downs, I think 'idyllic' applies."

"Tell me what, in particular, about your childhood makes you use the word 'idyllic'?"

"Well, Sammie and I had two loving parents, and not all of our friends did. Our homelife was, for the most part, happy and conflict-free. Sammie and I have always been great friends, and we had all the typical childhood experiences: We went to church regularly; Sammie and I both played sports; we had good schools and did well academically; our folks truly love and respect each other; and they love us unconditionally."

"Tell me about sports."

"Volleyball. Softball. Gymnastics—well, gymnastics until I turned thirteen, anyway. I grew like five inches in junior high. By the time I was a high school sophomore, I was too tall to be a gymnast. I loved the sport, but after I grew and my center of gravity shifted, I couldn't compete at the same level as my peers."

"How good were you before you grew too tall?"

Laynie laughed. "Pretty darned good—but after I topped five foot seven, I about tore my head off on the uneven bars. I switched to track, swim team, and cheering in high school."

"Okay. Now talk to me about church."

"What do you want to know?"

"Oh, what kind of church it was and how involved you were."

"It's a Bible-teaching Christian church. We attended worship every Sunday. Sammie and I went to Sunday school, summer camp, and vacation Bible school, and youth group on Friday evenings through high school."

"So, it was a fundamentalist church as opposed, say, to a liberal theology church concerned more with social welfare than rigid standards?"

"Not exactly. Although our church taught a literal interpretation of the Bible, we were also community oriented, and we participated in outreach programs. Our family helped local charities, such as homeless shelters and food pantries, and Sammie and I went on mission trips to Mexico."

Dr. Silverman watched Laynie's response to her next question. "And how do your present values line up with what you describe as 'a literal interpretation of the Bible'?"

Laynie recognized a trap when she heard one. The gynecologist's words fresh in her mind coupled with her own lack of commitment to her parents' faith guided her reply.

"I am my own person, Dr. Silverman. I'm flexible and adaptive. I make choices based on what is best and expedient at the time." *Like I'm doing right now.*

Dr. Silverman smiled her approval and jotted a note. While Laynie watched her write, that old, familiar whisper popped up.

Very good, Laynie. No sense shackling yourself to fanciful, unrealistic tenets and antiquated values.

CHAPTER 3

LP

SUNDAY MORNING, the candidates' exams flipped into a new phase. They ate breakfast early and, while the morning was still cool, Trammel gathered them together and drove them down the driveway. When they reached the fork in the drive, he veered right and conveyed the candidates through and beyond the trees that had blocked the view to what Laynie figured was the "real" campus.

She was right.

A two-story building that looked like a hotel surrounded by a parking lot occupied the first area on the left; on the right were many other and varied buildings and more parking spaces. Their vehicle passed the buildings and motored up the road until Laynie saw two obstacle courses, also on the left. One course appeared long and complex; the other was, at first glance, shorter and simpler.

Their vehicle pulled over to the courses, and Trammel ordered the candidates out. When Laynie got out, she looked farther down the road. Several hundred yards in the distance, off the road to the right, she made out a shooting range with positions for twelve or more shooters at a time. She counted two dozen or so individuals beneath the long roof that shaded the shooters' positions. A red flag waved from the flagpole on the corner of the lot. She heard the same distinctive popping sounds she'd heard on her arrival, but louder, because they were closer.

Farther to the left of the range, set far back from the road, was a very different structure. It looked like a big, rambling, single-story house but the structure was open to the sky. Instead of a roof, metal steps on the exterior led up to observation scaffolding that followed the outline of the building.

"Cool."

She hadn't spoken aloud to anyone in particular, but Black nodded his agreement.

"Shoot house. To practice breaching and clearing a building."

Black was tall and muscular with a square, superhero's chin and amber eyes. *A jock.* Laynie should know—she'd cheered for squads of them in high school.

He motioned with his blocklike, Dudley Do-Right chin. "And look there."

Laynie squinted. Beyond the range and shoot house, where the road looked like it ended but actually made an abrupt left-hand turn, set far back from the road, she saw . . . a city street? With a drug store and a bank and apartments? And more behind that?

"What is that?"

"Not sure. It looks like some kind of an urban mock-up. Maybe for realistic tactical or tradecraft training?"

Red mouthed, "'Bout to get real, huh?"

It was the first real exchange among the three of them since they'd arrived.

Laynie glanced at Red, wondering how her short, lithe body would perform on the obstacle course. The woman had glossy ebony hair cut in a bob; her pixie face and winking hazel eyes full of mirth and good humor put Laynie in mind of a leprechaun.

Trammel joined a man dressed in fatigues waiting by the simpler and shorter obstacle course and called the candidates over.

Trammel pointed at the man in fatigues. "This is Gunnery Sergeant Mays—just Gunny to you. He will put you through this course multiple times. I will observe."

Laynie shot another look at the course. *Should be entertaining.*

"You may notice personnel and trainees while on this side of the campus. You are to ignore them and keep your eyes on the tasks at hand. Understood?"

"Yes, sir," Laynie, Black, and Red replied.

For the next hour, Gunny ran them through the simple obstacle course one after another, again and again, recording their individual times. Then he pushed them. "Faster. Beat your own time by ten seconds your next two times through."

Laynie felt herself snap into a trance-like state. She had run the course three times and had retained each phase of the course: how many tires her long stride required her to step through, how many and how high the hurdles, the length of the crawl under metal girders, the number of steps across the beam over a pond of mud, how many monkey rings, and so on—up, over, across cargo nets, walls, and a swaying suspension bridge with no rails, also over mud.

Without planning to, she mentally drew a poster for each obstacle and pinned the posters in sequence. When Gunny blew the whistle, she bounded through the first obstacle, discarding the imagined poster for the next one. She poured on speed, pushing herself faster while maintaining the rhythm she needed to navigate each problem she'd already solved in her head.

When she finished the course, Gunny snapped his watch. "Eighteen seconds under your last run, Green. I think you can do better."

"Daaaang," Red muttered.

At the end of that hour, Gunny moved them to the second field. "This course will test team problem-solving abilities and skills. To win at this course, you must operate as a unit and finish as a unit. If one of you falls behind, you *all* fall behind. This is an exercise in physical agility that also reveals underlying group and leadership dynamics."

As Laynie turned to study what she could see of the course's layout, two lines of men and women jogged by. Out of the corner of her eye, she noticed not one remarkable thing about them—which may have been the point. They were dressed in generic running shorts and an eclectic variety of t-shirts; neither their hair nor clothing identified them as a unit. They were "normal." Ordinary. Inconspicuous. Only their faces, set in the same determined lines, told Laynie they were Marstead trainees.

I'll be one of you soon, Laynie promised them.

"Eyes front!" Gunny hollered. "You have one minute to strategize."

Laynie returned her attention to the formidable course. It began with a series of objects the team had to carry or maneuver over and under multiple barriers. Then they faced a high, wooden wall. Beyond that she spied a complicated ropes course that ran up into the trees.

She looked at Black and Red. "We ready for this?"

Black asked, "How about we take a quick team inventory? What are our strengths and limitations?"

He was looking at Red.

Red put her hands on her hips. "Sure, I'm shortest and probably weakest. Like, I can't heft that log over there and you probably can."

Laynie nodded. "Yeah, but you didn't get here on your good looks, right? What are your strengths?"

Red liked the question and grinned. "I'm agile as a monkey." She sniffed at Black. "Bet I can climb a rope faster than either of you."

Black shrugged. "All right. So, how do we want to do this?"

Laynie again studied what they could see of the course. "What if we agree that each obstacle or set of objectives needs a different approach? That means we shouldn't lock in on any particular strategy but adapt as needed. Carrying that first log? How about I lead; Red in the middle; you, Black on the end. But when we have to pull and push those big sandbags through the maze under those girders? The one of us who has the best pulling power should go first."

"Guess that's me," Black said.

"And we'll push. Now, on the ropes course, Red may have the advan—"

Gunny blew the whistle, ending their planning session. They lined up and, when Gunny blasted the whistle again, they hustled, Laynie and Black shouldering most of the weight of a heavy, cumbersome log over a four-inch-wide beam that zigged and zagged. When they dropped the log at the next obstacle, Black scooted, feet first, on his stomach, under the girders and grabbed hold of the mammoth sandbag they had to convey through the maze. Laynie and Red dove onto their bellies and pushed while Black pulled until they reached the other side.

Ahead of them loomed the wall.

Fifteen feet, Laynie estimated.

"How do we get you two up and over?" Black asked.

"Stand back, while I make a stirrup."

"You don't need to lift me; I'm pretty sure I can sprint toward it, jump, and catch the edge."

"It's not for you. I'm going to throw Red; then you're going to throw me."

"Oh yeah?"

Laynie stood with her back to the wall and her fingers intertwined. "Red, take a run?"

"You bet."

While Red strode back, Laynie called, "Black, watch us; you'll need to do the same for me."

Red was coming, as fast as she could run, the intense, measured stride of a gymnast. When she put her foot into Laynie's hands, Laynie launched her up, canted toward the wall. Red was ready; she flew like an arrow into the air, reached for the top of the wall, caught it, and hauled herself up with ease.

"Now me, Black."

Seconds later, Laynie was atop, then she and Red dropped to the ground on the other side. Black quickly followed.

"You okay, Green?"

"Scraped my elbow going over, but I'm fine."

"You're kind of dripping," Red pointed out.

Laynie swiped the blood off her arm and flung it aside. "Let's go."

They donned harnesses for the ropes course: a vertical cargo net climb up to the first platform (clip on to the safety cable); three short spans of hanging rings, rings that each of them had to swing/return to the person behind once they'd reached the swaying boards between the spans, until everyone reached the second platform (clip off, then clip on to the next safety cable).

Next came a fifteen-foot rope ladder up to the third platform (clip off, clip on); then a long, one-inch beam to the fourth platform with vertical hanging guide ropes that had to be swung to the person behind as they progressed (clip off, clip on); followed by a downward-sloping single-rope walk with other ropes as "bannisters" descending to the fifth platform (clip off, clip on).

A twenty-foot knotted-rope climb took them to the sixth platform (clip off, clip on); a suspension bridge of swaying wooden planks led to the seventh platform (clip off, clip on); a climb across *and* up a series of thin walls, hanging vertically, made from heavy-duty plastic with differing-sized holes for hand and foot purchases. The hanging walls took them to the eighth platform (clip off, clip on) and to a beam overhead that stretched across to the next platform—a beam with dowels protruding from its sides as handholds for them to swing across to the ninth platform (clip off, clip on).

The second-to-last obstacle was the most difficult challenge they'd encountered. They faced a two-story climbing wall to reach the tenth platform. The wall sported a wild diversity of handholds and footholds including rungs, "rock outcroppings," bars, and the odd mechanized purchase protruding from the wall.

A staff member clipped them to safety cables above, but he also joined the team's harnesses together, side by side, which required them to climb three abreast. That was the complication: The handholds and footholds were spaced apart in such a way that Laynie, Black, and Red had to climb up and over each other, staggering their progress, confounding their problem-solving skills. All that plus the discovery they made that, when someone stepped on a mechanized foothold, the mechanized handhold above it withdrew into the wall—a particularly unnerving experience for the individual clinging to the handhold as it retracted.

The point was, if one person fell, he or she would likely pull the other two off the wall.

"Well, crud." This from Black.

"*So* much fun," was Laynie's contribution.

After struggling upward about six feet, the three of them were tiring.

"We're never going to make it all the way up," Red whispered.

In her heart, Laynie agreed. "We need a different strategy, a different methodology. What if . . . what if we try this? Black, you and I huddle up and share every move. You step, I step. You grab, I grab?"

"What am I? Chopped liver?" Red exclaimed.

"No, you're the monkey, remember? You're going to ride on our backs."

"You've got to be joking." This came from Black, but Red was equally doubtful.

"She weighs, what? A buck ten? If we loosen the waistbands of our harnesses and she puts a toe inside each waistband, standing between us, we'll share her weight, and she'll keep us tethered together."

Black sized her up. "The waistband, right? Cause if you put your foot inside my leg strap, I'll be singing soprano long before we get to the top."

Red flicked an eyebrow. "I might pay real money to hear that."

The three of them snickered.

Red then devised an improvement to Laynie's idea. "What if I put my toe in the carabiner loop hanging from the waistbands of your harnesses?"

Black shot a hand into the air. "*That.* I vote for *that.*"

Red climbed onto Laynie and Black's bent thighs, and balanced there while she wedged the toe of her shoe into their carabiner loops.

"My feet are gonna tell me what-for tonight," she moaned.

"Just keep your weight leaned into the wall and use your hands to keep us anchored to the wall. We should move quickly once we're configured."

And they did. With Black and Laynie choosing their footholds and handholds together and advancing by sometimes standing on each other's feet, they made it to the top in another five minutes.

"That was brilliant," Red admitted. "Now let's get this done. I'm beat—and parched."

Black zip-lined to the ground and grabbed the rope pulley that returned the zipping apparatus to the top for the next person. Laynie came down next; she and Black together pulled the mechanism up for Red.

They ran toward Gunny, toward the course completion point. As they dragged themselves across the finish line, Gunny snapped his watch, looked at it, and shouted, "Again!"

Red gaped. "Are you kidding?"

"This time with feeling," Black muttered, starting a reluctant jog toward the log lift.

"Come on!" Laynie shouted, passing him.

They ran the course a second time, improving their team approaches and overall time. By then, the morning had turned to noon. The heavy humidity made their exercise miserable and exhausting.

They sprawled on the grass, sweating, aching, lungs heaving.

"Hydrate!" Gunny roared.

Laynie was almost too tired to eat when they returned to the lodge. She forced herself to chew and swallow half a sandwich. The rest of the lunch period, she nursed a bottle of water, five blisters, and her scraped elbow and forearm.

At the end of the meal, Trammel stood up. "The next two hours will be spent in what we call the Game Room. You'll participate in a timed round where you attempt to solve ten different puzzles and logic problems within the time allotted. For the final exam of the day, we'll evaluate your language skills and aptitude. Bonus? The Game Room is air-conditioned."

He cleared his throat. "I wanted to make one observation before we get back to work. We run this candidacy exam every other weekend, six months out of the year, usually with four candidates. On Pandora's Wall, we run two teams of two, each team tethered together, but it's not uncommon for one candidate to scrub out before then.

"When that happens, we tether the three candidates together, like we did with you. Nine-out-of-ten three-person teams do not complete the ropes course their first time through. They get stuck on Pandora's Wall. Your solution was one of the most ingenious I've seen, and it displayed great teamwork and trust."

The three of them nodded at his accolade. Black glanced at Laynie and started to say something, but the toe of Laynie's shoe connected his shin—*hard*—before he got his mouth open. He glared at her for an instant, then pursed his lips and nodded.

Message received: No one person should receive credit for a team's success.

THE GAME ROOM *was* air-conditioned—a relief after their workout in the morning's heat and humidity.

"Heavenly," Red breathed.

Three proctors greeted them, and each proctor took a candidate under their supervision. Trammel explained the process.

"You will complete a circuit of ten puzzles, brainteasers, or logic problems—ten differing types and of varying difficulty. Each puzzle has an allotted max completion time. Your proctor will start you at a station within the circuit, and you will progress through the circuit until you have completed all ten stations.

"Your proctor will record your time-to-completion or record your failure and will make notes on the approach you took to solve the puzzle. Take your places now."

Laynie's proctor led her to the fourth puzzle in the circuit. Red was several stations ahead of her; Black was behind. Laynie had never had a particular interest in puzzles. She was suddenly concerned that she might fail.

And fail she did.

She could not solve the Rubik's cube and came within a few seconds of finishing a slide puzzle—both fails. After two more similar physical brainteasers, Laynie was beginning to despair.

Then came the logic problems, similar to math problems like the train going seventy miles an hour for twenty-seven miles to reach town versus a car going fifty-six miles an hour for thirteen miles: Who reaches town first? Similar, but more insidious.

The Game Room's logic problems were conundrums, such as, "A mother, a father, and two children need to cross a river. They find a boat nearby, but it is small and can carry either one adult or two children at any one time. Both children are good rowers, but how can the whole family reach the other side of the river?"

Laynie's mind slipped into a gear similar to the one when she'd run the obstacle course. She saw the dilemma clearly—and the solution appeared as easily. She scrawled her answer: "The children row together from the near shore to the far shore; one gets out, the other returns. One adult rows to the far shore, and the child on the far shore rows the boat back to the near shore. Both kids then row across, and only one returns to the near shore. The other adult rows across and the child on the far shore rows back to the near shore. Both children then row across to the far shore."

She put her pencil down. "Done."

Her proctor clicked her stopwatch and made notes.

Laynie moved on to five other logic problems, solving each one within the allotted time.

Interesting.

THE LANGUAGE ASSESSMENT after that was also enlightening. She read aloud in Spanish, German, Swedish, and French, then conversed with four native speakers, each a trained linguist.

"Well, you'll never have to worry about passing as a native French woman," the French linguist laughed.

"I know. My accent is horrible. In my defense, I only took two years in high school before switching to German, whereas I took four years of Spanish and then chose Spanish and German for my college minor studies."

"For only two years of French study, you have a strong vocabulary and a nice grasp of French syntax—just not a great accent."

"Thanks."

Her Spanish linguist was more enthusiastic. "You have a facility and an ear for Spanish that seems to go beyond a second language. Have you done immersion study in a Spanish-speaking country?"

"No; took a month-long trip to Spain my senior year of high school, but that's it."

"Hmm. Did you spend time in a Spanish-speaking country during your language acquisition stage?"

"Um, what is that, exactly?"

"The ages in which children form and acquire their native languages, generally, one to five years old."

"I don't think so, but I was adopted at three, and I don't know where I lived before that."

"I see." The linguist made some notes that Laynie wished she could read.

I have no memories before Mama and Dad adopted us. Except for Care.

Another thought occurred to her. *Did I randomly choose Spanish as my first foreign language? Or, because of earlier influences I don't remember, did it choose me?*

She shrugged. *Guess I'll never know.*

She did okay in her German language session, too, but it was the Swedish session that piqued her curiosity and reminded her of what her recruiters, Angela and Bert, had asked her.

"Laynie, is your family, by chance, of Scandinavian descent? I ask because you have classic Scandinavian features—the height, blonde hair, and blue eyes."

After her Swedish session, their questions seemed to take on new meaning.

Her Swedish linguist commented after their conversation, "While your grasp of the language is not deep, you have a lovely accent and inflection."

"My dad's grandparents spoke Swedish to him and his parents, and he spoke it to my brother and to me. Although I wasn't raised around them, my dad's accent must have rubbed off on me."

The linguist nodded. "Well, I am certain it will serve you well."

Serve me well? Is that an indication of where I might be assigned, if I'm selected?

When the language portion of their exam was complete, the candidates were returned to the lodge, where they dropped into the chairs around the unlit fireplace.

"Man, I feel like I've run a marathon," Black admitted.

Laynie agreed. "I'd say so!"

Red chipped in, "More like a decathlon."

"And we survived it," Black added.

"Survived it?" Laynie snorted. "We clobbered it."

They looked at each other and grinned.

DINNER THAT EVENING took on a lighter atmosphere. Black, Red, and Laynie laughed about their obstacle course adventures, and Trammel didn't discourage the banter that had developed between them.

Black chuckled, "Green, when you launched Red to the top of that wall? Like a javelin! I thought she was gonna fly right over."

Red grinned. "Ten years of gymnastics will do that for ya."

Laynie realized before the others did that Red had "overshared."

With that, and with no fanfare, their time was over.

Trammel glared at Red and stood. "Candidates, please return to your rooms, pack, and prepare to depart."

Black reacted first. "I understood we fly out tomorrow?"

"You do. However, to minimize your interactions, you will be driven this evening to separate hotels in Baltimore, then conveyed to your flights in the morning. "This is merely a precaution against the natural tendency to deepen your acquaintances. Please guard against that tendency. If you are selected, it is possible, although unlikely, that you will encounter each other again, but you must never, in the field or out, endanger another agent by acknowledging a prior connection. Such a gaffe could prove fatal.

"I will also remind you of the conditions of the NDA you signed. Please review and commit to memory the verbiage we provided to you to describe both Marstead and this weekend's activities."

Trammel's mouth widened into a smile—and Laynie thought the look incongruous after seeing nothing but his stern or implacable expressions for two days.

"You'll receive word from us in the near future regarding the status of your candidacy."

IT WAS CLOSE TO nine o'clock when Laynie put her feet up in the nondescript Days Inn room Marstead had reserved for her. Her thoughts were on the past seventy-two hours. She felt like a major shift had taken place within her—that the experience had, in a tangible way, altered her, focused her as nothing before had.

What will I do if Marstead doesn't choose me? She didn't like the idea at all; in fact, it disturbed her.

She was surprised when a knock sounded at her door. Alert and cautious, she stood, moved to the side of the door, and asked, "Who is it?"

"Wes Trammel, Miss Green."

She peered through the peephole. It was, indeed, Trammel.

She opened to him, but did not ask him inside.

"May I come in?"

She didn't feel comfortable asking him into her room; she also didn't feel she could refuse him. She stepped aside, and he entered.

"Please shut the door, and I'll make this quick."

Laynie closed the door.

"Miss Green, I'm happy to extend an offer from Marstead to continue the selection process for a position with us."

Something inside Laynie unwound. "Sir?"

"Your training session will take place here and will last fourteen weeks. If you pass and advance, as I suspect you will, you'll be issued a formal 'job offer' and shipped abroad for further training and immersion into the culture you'll operate in. The session won't start until the second week of August. Think you can keep yourself out of trouble for a couple months?"

"Yes, sir, but . . ."

"But?"

"I think I'll be bored, sir."

He laughed softly—again, the change in his demeanor incongruous to Laynie. "I believe it."

He walked to the door. "You'll receive a letter a week or two before the start of the session with your travel details. Keep a tight watch on what you say and do until we see you again—oh, and stay fit. Think of your upcoming training as boot camp. On steroids."

Before he opened the door to leave, Laynie spoke. "May I ask a question, sir?"

Trammel's good humor vanished, replaced by his usual cool reserve. "I suppose."

She framed her inquiry carefully. "A great deal of our orientation and training focused on discretion—how to keep ourselves and Marstead's unofficial business secret—and yet, Marstead does not promote every recruit to probationary agent status. Other than your threats, what's to keep a rejected individual, someone who bears a grudge, from blowing up the Marstead organization?"

One side of Trammel's mouth tipped up. "Marstead is a legit business with its books and activities in perfect order, Miss Green. If our 'front' were somehow compromised, Marstead would persist as a successful business entity and continue to support our work financially. It is our network of trained intelligence officers that must be preserved, which is why we insist upon and enforce personal anonymity—and why it would prove difficult for a disgruntled trainee to do us real damage.

"However, as I mentioned earlier, not every employee works directly for Marstead. If Marstead ever came under too much scrutiny, we are prepared to relocate our operatives to contingency cover organizations. The relocation process would, no doubt, prove disruptive to our work, but not catastrophic."

He paused, then added, "Besides which . . . although our program does not lie under Congressional oversight, one should not make the mistake of assuming we don't have significant and powerful 'top cover,' cover that provides us with a high degree of safety and security. I would not, therefore, minimize the potency of our 'threats,' as you call them, Miss Green. I assure you: They are quite effective."

Staring at her, he asked, "Anything else?"

"No, sir. Thank you for setting my mind at ease."

CHAPTER 4

LP

LATE THE NEXT AFTERNOON, a cab dropped Laynie in front of her parents' home. She paced up the walkway to the front porch, suitcase in hand.

My parents' home. It wasn't, she realized, her home for much longer, and it occurred to her that, in her heart and mind, she'd already spread her wings. Had already left the nest.

She let herself in the front door. "Hello? I'm back!"

"Laynie! Laynie-girl!" Mama rushed from the kitchen to hug her. "Missed you so much."

"Me, too, Mama." Except she'd been too busy, run off her feet, to miss anyone.

"Dad will be home from work soon, sugar. You unpack and clean up, then we'll have a nice talk and you can tell me all about your trip."

"Yeah. Okay, Mama."

While she showered, Laynie rehearsed the boilerplate verbiage she was required to use to describe her weekend. It was, in all honesty, a pack of lies.

I must grow accustomed to prevaricating, to doing so without conscience or scruples, even to the point of believing my own stories. I'll be of no use if I can't lie convincingly.

OVER DINNER, LAYNIE told Polly, Gene, and Sammie about meeting other sales candidates Marstead was considering, regaled them with tales of Marstead's U.S. offices in Baltimore, of long briefings that covered all fifteen international offices, the company's hierarchy, and the different technology product branches.

Gene and Polly were politely attentive; Sammie seemed . . . mystified.

"What comes next, Laynie?" her dad asked.

"Well, they have invited me back for training."

"What kind of training?"

"Overall training in the company's technology branches—aeronautics, robotics, integrated circuitry manufacturing, telecommunications, information technology, R&D, application development, tech transfer protocols, science policy, and governmental policy—then specialized training within the branch I would be representing. The list of possibilities is pretty long, and if I do well on the training, Marstead has promised me a job. I can apply for my preferred branch, but they have the final say."

"And this is what you want to do, sugar?" Polly asked, confused by the many lofty and foreign terms Laynie had thrown out. "All this-here technology business?"

"I think it is, Mama."

Sammie's brow crinkled; he shook his head minutely, then slowly swiveled a penetrating gaze to confront his sister.

He isn't buying it.

Laynie dropped a veil over her expression. "Say, I'm hoping we can still take that ocean sailing class this summer like we planned, Sam."

In hopes that Marstead would invite her to their training program but not knowing when the training would start, Laynie had applied for and been hired as a substitute lifeguard with the city before the exam weekend. It was a flexible, part-time position, four or five hours an afternoon filling in at public pools wherever a full-time guard was out due to illness or other reasons. Lifeguards were in high demand, and she'd worked as a lifeguard for the city through previous summers. The city's hiring department was happy to get her back, even in a limited capacity.

Sammie, following in Laynie's footsteps, had taken a full-time summer job as a lifeguard. He had arranged his weekly schedule to have Fridays off so that they could take the sailing class she'd referred to.

They had both belonged to their high school's sailing club, learning sailing basics on the many inland waterways and lakes dotting the area around Seattle, then crewing on larger crafts on Lake Union. They wanted to grow their skills until they could expertly pilot a two-man boat out on Puget Sound. Sammie, in particular, nurtured the dream of owning a boat of his own.

"I'm still up for it . . . if you are."

"Sure I am. Why wouldn't I be?" Laynie had the sense that the moment they were alone, Sammie would start digging at her story, trying to pick apart the load of baloney she'd fed him and their parents—particularly because of the stultifying mumbo-jumbo she'd described. She needed to be ready to diffuse his suspicions.

Laynie went to work the next day, filling in as a relief lifeguard at a nearby pool. She worked Wednesday and Thursday, too, going wherever they needed a substitute, which had her hopping from one area of Seattle to another. In the mornings, before she left for work, she took Trammel's words on fitness seriously: She ran two miles at sunup and arrived at the pool to swim laps before it opened to the public.

On Friday, she and Sammie drove together to start the ocean sailing course at a marina on Lake Union. They hadn't been in the car five minutes before, as Laynie suspected he would, Sammie started in.

"How'd you scrape your arm, Laynie?"

"Hmm? What?"

"When you came home Monday, you had that scrape on your elbow and forearm. Didn't get that in a briefing on 'governmental policy,' did you?"

"Of course not. Marstead put on a picnic Sunday afternoon—one of those 'welcome to the Marstead family' things. Part of it was a team-building exercise, this sort of an obstacle course we all had to run. Guess I'm sort of a klutz, 'cause I scraped my arm going over one of the walls."

Laynie was fabricating, going off script, but convincingly so.

She hoped.

Sammie, in the passenger seat, turned toward her. "Okay. It's just that . . . this new fascination with Marstead seems, I dunno, out of character for you."

Laynie had to reply with just the right amount of firmness. "In what way?"

"I guess I can't see you as a geek?"

She came on a littler stronger, a smidge indignant. "Is that how you see me? As a geek?"

"No, that's exactly how I *don't* see you. You're too active and too smart—I don't mean brainiac smart, but insightful smart. And politically smart. I mean, what are you doing with a tech firm when you have a poli-sci degree?"

"Believe it or not, little brother, I'm really jazzed by how technology can affect the political climate in the world." She threw in a huffy breath for good measure.

He nodded and didn't answer until, minutes later, in a gruff voice, he pronounced, "Yeah, well, you've never been a klutz in your life."

Chapter 5

LP

ON MONDAY, the first of August, Laynie received her letter from Marstead containing the instructions regarding her training. She read it, memorized it, then shredded it by hand and flushed the dissolvable paper down the toilet—not that the contents of the letter would have meant much to the uninitiated reader. She gave her notice to the city the following morning.

Sunday afternoon, she again flew into BWI. Her instructions this time required that she locate a Trailways bus outside the Arrivals area, a bus bearing the markings "Dunlop Travel" on the sides. Laynie found the bus—it wasn't difficult—and noted that the bus's windows were darkened so that no one could see inside.

She presented herself at the bus door to the official wearing a Dunlop Travel uniform.

"Name?"

"Pitcher. Molly."

It was a code word. Molly Pitcher had been an alias assigned to protect another woman's identity, a woman said to have fought in battle alongside men during the American Revolution. The alias was to protect the brave woman's true identify from the British—who would have hanged her. "Molly Pitcher" also became a generalized sobriquet for women who carried water to men on the battlefield during the war.

Laynie wondered what code name the male trainees had been given to use.

The man rifled through his sheets on the clipboard, found her photograph, studied it, and compared the likeness to her face.

He spoke quietly, so that only she heard his orders. "Board the bus and take the available seat closest to the back. We'll be parked for another hour, until all the flights arrive. No talking, please; the rules of anonymity are in effect."

He jerked his chin to another uniformed man loading luggage to take charge of her suitcase and overnight bag.

Laynie stepped onto the bus, excited to return to Marstead's campus, excited for what she'd learn in the weeks to come. The bus's interior was dim, and Laynie couldn't see far into the back. Light principally came from the narrow, above-the-seat lamps.

She took an aisle seat next to a woman appearing to be a few years older than her. They nodded, took each other's measure, but obeyed the rule of silence.

Like her seatmate, Laynie drew a book she'd been reading on the plane from her handbag and used it to distract herself.

An hour and fifteen minutes later, they were on their way. An hour after that, the bus ground to a stop, its diesel engine idling. Laynie could see little through the darkened windows—just enough to know they were stopping at the gate to the Marstead compound. Minutes later, they rolled through, taking the left fork up the drive.

She strained to see the campus unfold before her and was not surprised when the bus pulled into the parking lot in front of the "hotel" Laynie had noted during her exam weekend.

"Ladies and gentlemen, we have arrived. Please gather your things, disembark, and collect your luggage."

When Laynie stepped from the bus, it was early evening in Maryland. She had lost three hours flying across the country, another hour waiting for the bus to load, another in transit. She was standing to the side, waiting for her luggage, when a brawny arm wrapped itself around her waist and squeezed her.

She jerked and turned, encountering the smirking face and square chin of Black. She grinned and hugged him back—only to have a third person horn in on them: Red.

The three of them hugged and thumped each other's backs, and Laynie laughed softly and whispered a, "Yay us!"

"Yes, *hooray!*" Red repeated with the same quiet jubilation.

Theirs was not the only reunion. Around them a few others found their exam companions and shook hands or hugged as they did.

Then Trammel appeared and blew his whistle. "I know you're finding old pals among our ranks, and that is fine—provided you maintain identity anonymity. You have each been issued a training alias that you'll find in your room, a first name only. Until then, feel free to use your previous color names—keeping in mind the likelihood that more than one trainee will answer to those colors."

Twenty-nine trainees laughed at Trammel's little joke, but Laynie just shook her head.

Trammel joking? Pretty sure I see pigs flying overhead—and the hot place may have just dropped below freezing.

"Green, I had no doubt I'd find you here," Black exclaimed. "Just wasn't sure I'd be here with you."

"Nah. I knew the three of us were a lock."

Still happy and exchanging banter, they gathered their bags and headed into the "hotel."

The trainees' barracks operated much like a hotel, too. At the front desk, trainees were identified by their photographs and issued single rooms. Laynie and her friends, once in possession of their keys, separated to find their quarters—and their new names for the next three and a half months.

Laynie unlocked the door and stepped into her room. She put her suitcase on the bed, wandered in and out of the bathroom, and stood at the window, checking out her "view." She was on the back side of the hotel. Beyond the asphalt that ran around the building, rugged, forested acreage greeted her and, through the trees, the daunting line of the security fence.

Laynie unpacked her suitcase into her room's dresser. She'd brought what her letter had advised her to bring—multiple pairs of shorts and sweatpants, long- and short-sleeved t-shirts, a heavy sweatshirt, a rain slicker. Two pairs of quality running shoes. Lots of durable socks. Mosquito and tick repellent. Her own supply of bandages and antiseptic ointment.

Must think we'll have blisters galore.

On the dresser she spotted a plain, unsealed envelope. Within it was a slip of paper bearing the single word, "Magda."

Laynie guffawed. "Magda, huh? Well, all right."

She thought a moment. "Maggie. I like Maggie better."

A LATE DINNER WAS scheduled for 8:00 in the dining hall across the road from the hotel. Laynie entered and counted ten round tables ranged around the dining hall—including a table of six where Trammel, Gunny, and four other staff members sat and where, at the tables alongside them, additional staff members waited.

Two staff tables in particular caught Laynie's eye: a group of men and women—seasoned, hardened, and dressed uniformly in camo pants and dark beige polo shirts.

Laynie skirted the room when she spied Black and Red waving. They were holding a seat for her. She noticed that the trainee tables seated five.

Black stood and offered his hand. "Hey there. I'm Chuck. You can call me *Chuck*. You know, short for *Chuck*."

Laynie raised one brow, pursed her lips, and shook her head in disappointment. "And here I thought sure it'd be Dudley—or should I say, *Dud*. You know, just *Dud*, as in short for *Dudley*."

The three other trainees at their table groaned; Laynie bit back a guffaw.

Chuck's eyes narrowed. "So, that's how it's gonna be, is it?"

Not to let Laynie's playful razzing go unchallenged, he stroked his prominent chin. "Well, I guess they didn't want to *do right* by me."

The table sided with Chuck, hooting and pointing at Laynie.

"Oh my, that's *terrible*, but I did start it," Laynie admitted, grinning. She added, "They gave me Magda. Please call me Maggie. *Please*. I'm too young to be a Magda."

Chuck patted her back. "You got it, Maggie. I'll let the rest of the table introduce themselves."

Red grinned. "I like it. Maggie beats Green any day. I'm Stephanie, by the way."

"Hey, Stephanie. Love what you've done with your hair."

Stephanie's glossy black hair was shorter, bluntly cut and slung along her sharp cheekbones. "No muss, no fuss for running obstacle courses on hot, muggy days."

Laynie pointed to her long hair. "Yeah. I brought a supply of ponytail ties. This mop on my neck in this heat? No thanks."

Laynie's seatmate from the bus smiled. "I've been baptized Nora, and this young stud is the newly minted Taylor. Oh, and yes, I also had my bob trimmed up for this."

Nora's accent was unmistakably British.

Taylor ran a hand over his blonde, freshly buzzed flattop. "I brought *my*, er, ponytail holders, too." His English was excellent, and he managed to keep a straight face while his table mates chuckled.

Swedish? Norwegian? Not sure. Definitely Scandinavian, though, Laynie thought.

Chuck couldn't resist advising Taylor. "Well, don't sweat it, Taylor. If you break ponytail thingies, Maggie will lend you one of hers. Gotta keep that mop off your neck, bro."

His quip elicited further laughs from the table.

Laynie extended her hand to Nora and Taylor. "Pleased to meet you both; I'm really glad to be here."

The sentiment of the others was universal, and they shook hands all around. When a strident bell sounded at eight o'clock, those at the staff tables rose to get their dinner.

"Well, shall we get in line to grab some grub before it's gone?" Chuck asked.

Stephanie jumped up. "Starved. Let's go."

Everything was buffet style: lots of salads, fruits, and wholegrain breads, with two entrees to choose from. Tonight's entrees were baked fish and meatloaf. The buffet had light desserts, too. The five table mates loaded their plates—anticipating the heavy physical activity coming their way—and, between bites, talked about the only topic safe for them to discuss, the upcoming training.

At precisely 8:30, another bell sounded, and Trammel stood up.

"I want to congratulate you on your advancement to this phase of the selection process. We screen hundreds of candidates prior to the informal interview and hold exam weekends throughout the year. Since we run only two training sessions of thirty recruits a year, I think you can appreciate that your arrival here today is both an honor and an achievement in itself.

"That said, not all of you will survive the coming fourteen weeks, and I'll tell you why some of you won't. Since we have already examined your physical condition, mental health, language aptitude, and intelligence for this type of work, if you leave this process it will be for one reason only: *Someone* will have decided that you are not a good fit for the life we are asking you to live.

"Now, that 'someone' could be me or could be the consensus of the training staff, but it could also be you. As we progress through the curriculum, *you* may be the 'someone' who determines that this is not the life you've dreamed of. I ask you to be honest with yourself and with us. There's no shame in knowing yourself; rather, there is strength. If you arrive at the conclusion that this is *not* the path you choose to take, please come to me directly. We will process you out quietly and see you home. Again, no harm, no foul.

"Why do I begin your training with what some might consider a 'downer' of an introduction? Because, by the end of this week, two or more of you will be gone. That's the norm. The average 'graduation' rate from Alpha Field Training is fifty percent or less. That's right—at least fifteen out of the thirty of you in this room will not complete the training—generally one or two owing to serious injury, two or more by staff consensus, the remainder by choice.

"Bear my words in mind: The training will be hard, and it will challenge you, but the life ahead won't get any easier. Whether you have a sudden, grand epiphany or simply acknowledge that you are not suited for this life—by nature, choice, inclination, or moral scruples—be fair to yourself and to us."

He looked to his left. "Ms. Vickers will now detail our daily schedule."

The woman who rose to her feet beside Trammel looked to be in her fifties with a cap of short, iron gray hair. Her body language was rigid and formal; she referred to a clipboard that, Laynie decided, may or may not have been surgically attached to her body.

And the first words from her mouth told Laynie a lot. *Why, she's British.*

In the high, stiff tones of a good upper-crust British education, Vickers said, "Good evening trainees, and welcome. We have fourteen weeks with you to begin the process of molding you, teaching you, and, I believe, imparting to you the skills that may someday save your lives. I say *begin the process*, because if you propose to become an asset to the Company, you will view your stay here as only the foundation of your training.

"I cannot stress adequately enough how essential a proper mental attitude is. While I am glad to see you relaxed and socializing with your compatriots on our first evening, that must change. From this point forward, you must will yourselves to approach each day with the serious intent it requires.

"Mr. Trammel made mention of our fifty-percent dropout rate, that one or two trainees each session suffer serious injury. I would add this: In my thirty years of experience, nine out of ten instances of serious injury or death in the field may be traced to personal presumption, the failure of an agent to maintain the appropriate mindset."

As Vickers uttered the words, "death in the field," the room around Laynie stilled.

"Proper mental focus will be an ongoing topic; please prepare yourselves tonight to adopt the earnest mental mindset that will guard you and your mates tomorrow."

She shifted her gaze to the clipboard. "Now, on to what to expect day-to-day. Elements of your schedule will remain static while you are here: PT, 5:45 to 6:30 a.m.; breakfast, 7 to 7:30; lunch, noon to 1 p.m.; dinner, 6 to 6:30 p.m. We will hold a daily after action review in the briefing room following dinner.

"The AAR will last as long as is necessary. You will have free time following the AAR until ten o'clock, at which time, lights out."

She looked up from her clipboard and pointed at the cork board on the dining hall wall. "Daily activities and assignments will be posted on that board before breakfast each morning. Expect concentrated instruction in firearms, firearms tactics, and hand-to-hand combat. Near the end of this course, you will undergo Marstead's version of SERE fieldcraft—survival, evasion, resistance, and escape. Our SERE experience will not rise to the level of special operations training, but it will equip you with vital basics.

"You will learn tradecraft—aspects of surveillance, intelligence gathering, and covert communications. I advise you to learn well if you wish to remain alive in the field. Your day's tradecraft activities will be a mix of classroom principles and their application, case studies and exercises, physical undertakings that will evolve into combined sorties. These maneuvers will begin simple but graduate to complex activities that will test your skills, endurance, mettle, and loyalties."

She turned to the table. "Gunny?"

Laynie had spent half a day under Gunny's "tender" direction—four hours that had left her sore for a week. She unconsciously sat up straighter.

"You will gather for PT at 5:45 a.m. sharp each morning at the flagpole outside these doors. Wear shorts, shirts, good shoes, good socks. My assistants lead PT, and they start on time.

"You can expect warm weather this time of year, although it will be cooling over the next month; you should expect to also see rain. Rain or shine, you will run two miles before breakfast. If you are late to start, you will run four miles. Sadly, breakfast ends at 7:30, so should you miss PT with the other trainees, I'm certain you'll wish you'd been on time and won't repeat your mistake.

"Two doors down, attached to the gymnasium, is the commissary where you may, during the noon hour or the hour prior to dinner, purchase beverages, snacks, and sundry necessities such as toothpaste, socks, and hygiene products. We grant you two dollars in commissary credit each day; use cash for additional purchases.

"Next door to the commissary is the logistics shack. After we dismiss this evening, you'll line up at Logistics to draw boots, hat, and rangewear in your size—fatigue trousers and long-sleeved shirts—from the supply officer. If you need replacements for any of these items during training, see the supply officer during commissary hours."

Gunny gestured to the next two tables and the men and women wearing camo pants and polo shirts as uniforms. One of the men stood and surveyed the room.

"This is our rangemaster, Mr. Henry. Later this week, you'll become acquainted with our firearms instructors, armorers, and self-defense instructors.

"When, at range staff instruction, you draw your firearms and ammo, you will do so from the logistics shack, same place you'll draw your rangewear. You will learn the range rules during your first firearms class, but whenever you enter the range, you *will* wear your designated rangewear; you will also don eye and ear protection. You will never enter the range dressed otherwise. Understood?"

"Yes, Gunny," the trainees answered in unison.

"Right. Dr. Gupta is next."

Laynie remembered Dr. Gupta. *She's the gynecologist.* She also recalled the uncomfortable conversation they'd had.

"I am to speak on how we will maintain health and wellness during your training session. Injuries are common; most are relatively minor. Report any injury needing more than a bandage and antibiotic ointment to your nearest instructor. A paramedic is always on call and will come to evaluate you.

"The same goes for any rash or fever: If you have a rash or a fever, report it immediately. Infectious diseases, such as influenza and meningitis, thrive where men and women live and train in close proximity. You all recall where the clinic is from your exam weekend, yes?"

"Yes," they replied.

"Good; however, you are not to go to the clinic unaccompanied by a paramedic or an instructor. In fact, leaving the training grounds unaccompanied—the grounds are clearly delineated by wide yellow lines across the asphalt and grass and by the perimeter fence—will result in your dismissal from the program.

"If you are promoted to probationary agent status, you will, on the last day of the program, receive a series of vaccinations customized to your area of operation. You may suffer some ill effects—redness and tenderness at the injection sites and flu-like symptoms, such as fever and achiness, that may persist for up to three days.

"The side effects are why we wait to give the injections until the end of the program—so that we do not lose valuable training time while you recover—but also because immunity is not immediate. Since we do not give those injections now, we have chosen to mitigate the possibility of an infectious disease sweeping the campus by housing you in private rooms with your own showers.

"One more thing? After we dismiss and you draw your rangewear from the logistics shack, I would ask all female candidates to meet me in our daily briefing room, directly next door."

She looked around. "I believe Ms. Stridsvagn is next?"

Ms. Stridsvagn stood. The Stridsvagn name was Swedish. Perhaps in her late thirties, she was solidly built, blue-eyed, and dark-blonde. If not of Scandinavian heritage, she certainly looked the part.

Like me, Laynie thought.

However, when Ms. Stridsvagn opened her mouth to speak, Laynie's assumptions about her were confirmed: Laynie's father possessed the same lilting English accent—although much less pronounced, since he grew up speaking both English and Swedish.

Sweden seems to be well-represented here. Odd, considering Sweden is not a NATO signatory.

"I will repeat a word of warning regarding the staff and your fellow trainees. You have surely realized by now that not everyone on this campus is American. This stands to reason since Marstead is a global entity. However, I must also caution you, *yet again*, not to pry into your fellow trainees' backgrounds and not to, even in casual conversation, give up your own personal details or, if another trainee questions you, respond to those queries. In point of fact, if anyone, staff or otherwise, seeks to garner your identity or background information, please report them to myself or Mr. Trammel immediately.

"Mr. Olifant?"

The last staffer from the senior staff table stood. "Thank you, Ms. Stridsvagn."

He stood with his hands in his pockets, rocking back on his heels, quite casually. "Why? Why are we, on the issue of anonymity, careful to a fault? What is our point? Just this: If you complete your training and advance to probationary status, you will be assigned to a country of operation where you will assume a new identity.

"In the interests of ongoing operational security and for your own safety, your assumed identity must remain unknown to all—your fellow trainees, your family and friends, and those whom you've known in your previous life. Your 'previous life' must include the here and now.

Let me say it differently: This period of training is the buffer between your past and your future. Who you were *yesterday* must be sharply severed from who you become *in the field*. Only Marstead recruiters, HR, and upper management may ever know your true identity and origin.

"Again, why? I mentioned 'operational security' or OPSEC—that is, the protection and well-being of the operation itself and those involved in it. While all that is true, please consider other, further hazards a field operative may face.

"Should your cover be 'blown' in the field and your original ID uncovered? Your family and loved ones could become unwitting pawns leveraged against you in an international chess game between good and evil. Threats to their safety and well-being could be used to turn you, to force you to commit treason, to 'out' your fellow operatives, putting at risk field personnel all over the world.

"Aliases equal anonymity, and anonymity is your greatest protection—and ours. Do not compromise your anonymity or that of your fellow trainees in any manner. Remember, too, that although we take care not to assign fellow trainees to the same fields of operation, you may, someday, encounter one of your fellow trainees 'out there' in the great, big world. What you *do not know* about that individual can never be used to harm him or her—and vice versa."

He let his warnings sink in. "Anonymity is vital to your safety. Have I said enough on this topic?"

"Yes, sir," came the murmured response.

"You are dismissed."

Laynie and the other trainees beat a path to the logistics shack. As Gunny had said, it was past the gymnasium and the commissary, set off on its own. However, "shack" didn't do it justice. The building, while not large, was built of high-quality concrete and steel on a concrete foundation, with a thick door and a steel slide-up service window. Both the door and service window, Laynie imagined, would require a couple of grenades to breach.

The building's courtyard was, furthermore, surrounded by a twelve-foot perimeter fence topped with spotlights and loops of wicked-sharp razor wire. At the moment, the fence's gate was open, as was the service window. Trainees lined up in front of the window under the bright lights that illuminated the courtyard.

Behind the "shack," encompassed by the perimeter fence, sat a steel bunker.

"Ammo bunker," Chuck breathed in her ear. "Restricted access."

Laynie hadn't realized he'd followed her from the dining hall, but she was glad he had.

"Hey, Black."

"Chuck," he reminded her.

Laynie smiled. "Yeah, I know, but I think you'll always be Black to me—Black with the superhero chin, and *never* a Dud."

"Thanks. I think."

The wait per person was short: The supply officer had their rangewear packages preassembled and labeled. Laynie flashed back to the tech who'd taken her shoe size and measurements during exam week.

They think of everything, she marveled. *Been doing this a while, I guess.*

After she'd pulled her packaged gear—bound in a bundle made heavy by the box of boots on top, she headed back to the dining hall to find the briefing room.

She and eleven other women took seats at the long tables facing a podium. When Dr. Gupta entered, the female trainees stilled.

Dr. Gupta was not alone; with her was a nurse Laynie recognized. The nurse pushed a wheeled cart. Dr. Gupta addressed the women.

"I have called you here to discuss your sexual health. We have screened all the trainees for STDs, so you can be at ease on that score. And, since you are all adults; what you do on your off time is your business.

"However, an unplanned pregnancy is *our* business. We have invested quite a lot of time and money into your candidacy up to this point and will invest more with each day of training. If you were to fall pregnant, you would be dismissed from the program.

"Therefore, it is our policy to provide birth control for our female candidates. Your health profile will follow you wherever you go in Marstead; if you are operating in the field, your contraceptive implant will be updated as needed."

On her signal, the nurse held up what looked like a thin capsule.

"This will be implanted just beneath the skin of the inside of your upper arm. We'll inject a light numbing agent first, then inject the implant. It is quite painless and very efficient."

Laynie could not believe what she was hearing. Her gorge rose, and she was not the only woman in the room who objected to Gupta's precipitous—her cool, presumptive—manner.

A girl jumped up, both her voice and head shaking. "No. You don't have the right to do that. It's against my religion, and I'm not doing that."

Dr. Gupta nodded. "Very well. An instructor is waiting outside with a golf cart. He will accompany you to out-processing and arrange transport home for you."

The girl looked around, stunned, blinking her eyes. "That's it? No choice in the matter? No discussion or options?"

"I believe you signed and agreed to the policy that specifically gives Marstead control over any and all health procedures we deem necessary, did you not?"

The girl nodded, reluctantly.

"Please," Dr. Gupta pointed to the door, "Exit through there."

"But . . . well, what if I—"

"I'm sorry. You have been dropped from the program."

Laynie fumed. *Had to make an example of her, didn't you? Had to make sure we all took the rules seriously.*

Laynie understood the logic, but it didn't stop her from disliking Gupta more now than she had on their first meeting. At that moment, Laynie itched to get up and follow the flustered ex-trainee out the door. She slid her eyes around the room and saw she wasn't the only one considering the same thing. Steph stared at her hands. Nora glanced her way and shook her head.

That's a 'no' from Nora—although she's as ticked off as I am.

So, Laynie didn't leave.

Not because she wasn't angry, not because she wasn't brave enough, not because she didn't dislike Gupta's high-handed manner, but because, in spite of every good reason, she was willing to pay the price.

Well, what does this implant mean to me, anyway, other than a moment of discomfort? Am I going to throw myself into bed with some guy and rejoice, 'Gee, I'm so glad I have it?' Not likely, not even remotely.

The bottom line for Laynie was in the future: She wanted to finish the training, graduate, and advance to probationary status—and the bottom line was the only line Laynie wouldn't cross.

I don't much care what it takes to get through the training—as long as I get through it.

CHAPTER 6

LP

LAYNIE, DRESSED IN running gear, liberally dosed with mosquito repellent, a bandage covering a small entry point on her left, inner arm, was under the flagpole outside the dining hall at 5:35 the following morning. She hadn't slept soundly for a number of reasons but mostly out of fear her alarm would not wake her on time and she would be late.

She was not the only trainee early to the flagpole that morning. Just one person fell into line at the last possible moment—but no one was late.

Black, coming up beside Laynie, stepped in place to warm up his legs. "Did I hear right? We lost a trainee already?"

Laynie pressed her lips together and answered with a single, sharp nod.

"Let's go, people!"

In two lines, the trainees set off down the road, jogging lightly behind Gunny's two assistants, Júlio, and Hristo. They passed the gymnasium, commissary, and logistics shack on the right, obstacle courses on their left, then the firing range and the shoot house on their right. Set way back from the road where it took a sharp left, stood that sprawling, incongruous slice of town plunked down where a forest should have been standing.

Laynie got a better look at the "urban mock-up" as Hristo picked up the pace and they drew abreast of it, although it was still a thousand yards distant. From what she could see, it truly was a fake city, or at least two full blocks of it, complete with shops, offices, a market, a bank, a little park, and second-story apartments, knit together by two streets, several intersections, and alleys. It was built out far in a field where the trees had been cleared, set apart by itself. A single paved street intersected the road and led to town.

Laynie was not the only trainee scoping it out.

Whatever that's for, it's gonna be interesting.

"Come on, trainees!" Hristo shouted to pull their attention back.

She fastened her eyes on the backs of Júlio and Hristo's heads. *Hristo. What nationality it that? Belgian? And is Júlio a Mexican or Spanish name?* Like Sweden, neither Mexico nor Spain were NATO signatories—but Portugal was. *So, maybe Portuguese?*

But Sweden is not a NATO member, and we've got a Swede on staff, another Swede as a trainee, and the linguist during my exam weekend made a big deal about my dad's Swedish heritage and my having a working use of Swedish?

Not to mention, Bert bringing up my Scandinavian looks during our interview.

It was an odd mash-up of factual tidbits that Laynie pondered as the road looped around east and came back down the other side of the obstacle courses and hotel. The road's circuit delivered the trainees back to the dining hall parking lot and the flagpole.

"Line up! Five abreast!"

Hristo led them in a series of calisthenics and stretching for another twenty minutes.

"Okay," Júlio said to them. "Not bad; we'll add some steam to our run tomorrow. Today, go grab a shower and meet in the dining hall for breakfast at 7:00."

THEIR FIRST CLASS after breakfast, held in the classroom adjoining the briefing room, began at 8 a.m., marking the true start of Marstead's rigorous training program.

"I want you to understand the uniqueness of Marstead," their instructor, Mr. Chin, said by way of introduction. "It is this: Marstead is not a law enforcement agency, and you are not law enforcement officers. While we'll cover International Law as a necessary part of your tradecraft and you'll receive further instruction relative to the laws of your country of operation, I need to impress that distinction upon you now: You are not training to enforce the law. We do not report crimes or apprehend criminals. The reports we write are limited to what we accomplish and the intel we provide.

"What this means is that, technically, everything we do is off book. Yes, we're working under the joint sponsorship of the U.S. and NATO on behalf of the free world, and our objectives are to ensure that our world *stays* free, but how we do that is covert, behind the scenes, and often extralegal. Outside the scope of the law. Definitely without the knowledge of pertinent law enforcement organizations.

"We exist in broad daylight but operate in the shadows; we use the means and methods necessary to complete our assigned tasks, cutting out red tape and bureaucracies, skirting legalities and conventions. Yes, occasionally our field operatives land in hot water with local law enforcement. If that happens, Marstead will, in many instances, extricate you, but we will do it quietly and covertly. More on that later."

In many instances? More on that later? What if Marstead can't manage to "extricate us?" What then?

"We will teach you how to conduct yourself and survive in the field—these often being one and the same."

He put his hands on his hips and surveyed the class. "The majority of you have seen no military training—and we like it that way. Why? Because our personnel should seem to be 'normal people' who blend in, and because it is hard, once trained to the military way, to drop the habits the military has drummed into you.

"For example, if you, as a trainee, are given an order to *jump* and you respond with, "Yes, sir; how high, sir?" and you can't break that habit? If you are wound too tightly and cannot change? You will fail this course."

Many trainees chuckled, but Laynie, seated to the left of Stephanie, then Black, slid her eyes toward Black. His brow was furrowed.

Will it be too hard for him to break those responses? Laynie wondered.

"We'll begin with the basics of covert communications in the field."

Chin talked about brush passes, dead drops, and coded messages such as one-time pads, key-encrypted ciphers, and crossword puzzles or word scrambles published in newspapers. "Each of these tried and true communication methods has an infinite number of variations. Let's watch a training film and discuss what we observe."

He dimmed the lights and ran a reel loaded onto a projector. The three-minute film was of a crowded subway station, taken from across the tracks, looking down on the waiting, jostling passengers. Laynie's eyes darted back and forth across the packed platform, but she caught nothing out of the ordinary.

The film ended, and Chin, without turning on the lights, asked, "What did you see?"

Silence. No one in the class had an answer.

"Let's watch it again. This time, look for and note two individuals—the woman with the green hat and the man with a folded newspaper under his arm."

He rewound and restarted the film, pausing it as the subway platform came into view. "I want you to find the two subjects before we continue. Lift your hand as soon as you've spotted them."

It took an entire minute for everyone to lift their hand. The woman was standing on the left side of the screen, near the edge of the platform. Her expression was bored and impatient. The man was behind the press of waiting passengers, far to the right of her, the newspaper clearly visible under his right arm.

Chin let the film run again. Without shifting his head, eyes, or expression, the man edged through the crowd, until he was directly behind the woman. When the train arrived, she stepped forward to board. Laynie caught only a glimpse, but she was certain: The woman now had a newspaper under *her* arm. The man seemed to fall back from the crush of boarding passengers, yet naturally so. He moved down the platform and boarded using a different set of doors.

The film ended and the class exhaled. Laynie had leaned forward, mesmerized, because the couple on the film were amazing.

"It is as equally important to recognize a pass when it happens—such as the one you just witnessed—as it is to learn the skill yourself," Chin said.

He then ran other scenarios spliced into the film, stopping at each scenario to orient the class to what was about to happen, then to have them discuss what they'd seen. They spent an hour reviewing scenario after scenario.

After a break, he talked about dead drops and the signals involved. "A 'dead drop' or 'dead letter box' allows intel to be passed, agent to agent, without them ever meeting. The drop can be arranged for any time of day, reducing the possibility of either agent being detected.

"The elements of a drop are the location—where the drop exists—and the signals. The drop itself is a hiding place using a common, everyday location. The receiver must be able to retrieve the intel from the hiding place without being spotted.

"If you are the agent leaving intel in the drop, you have prearranged a signal with your receiver that tells him the drop is active. Conversely, you must have a signal that says the drop has been compromised—or burned. These signals are most often in plain sight, along the receiver's everyday route, so that he has only to pass by to see them."

Chin started a list on the chalk board. "A casement curtain or blind opened/closed or up/down, a houseplant set in a specific window, a porch or window light on or off, a wad of chewed gum stuck on the back of a stop sign, an advertisement on a public notice board."

Chin turned on an overhead projector and, from a folder, withdrew a transparency. When he laid the transparent "foil" on the projector's surface, a laundromat's bulletin board came into view. The board was stippled with business cards, scraps of paper asking for rides to certain towns, apartments for rent, even free kittens.

"See the Lost Dog notice? What can you tell me about it?"

A trainee spoke up. "It has ten phone number strips hanging from the bottom."

"What about those numbers?"

Laynie noticed it. "The fifth phone number strip from the left has two transposed digits."

"Very good." He replaced the transparency. It was the same bulletin board, but the strip with the misprinted phone number was missing.

"That's the signal? But what's to keep anyone from tearing off that strip?" someone asked.

"What do you think?" Chin asked.

"There is no 'Lost Dog,'" Stephanie suggested. "It's a fabrication, so who would tear off a phone number for a dog they haven't seen?"

"Good—if there *is* no 'Lost Dog,' the odds are miniscule that anyone would take one of the phone numbers. What else?"

"People don't generally tear from the center," another trainee said, "so tearing off the only misprinted number makes it a deliberate choice."

"Good catch! And this? What does this mean?"

Chin put up yet another transparency of the bulletin board. The same "Lost Dog" notice was there, but the top corner of the sheet of paper was dog-eared, turned down and creased.

Several trainees spoke at the same time. "Burned!"

"That's right. The sender has signaled the recipient that the drop has been compromised. They won't use the drop or that set of signals again. And this?"

Same board, but scrawled across the "Lost Dog" notice was the word, "Found."

"That's much more noticeable," someone said.

"If it is, what's the reason?" Chin asked.

"Danger," Laynie murmured.

"Who said that?"

"I did. It's a danger signal, perhaps a 'change location quick' or 'get out of town now' message."

"That's exactly what it is—all prearranged agent-to-agent. Now, let's look at another set of signals."

The next transparency showed an antique shop set on a corner, its front window display cluttered with vintage goods including an entire set of shelves filled with knickknacks.

"Good one," someone said. "Lots of possibilities."

"But obvious, don't you think?" Black asked. "It's like a signals smorgasbord."

Without comment, Chin replaced the transparency. Same corner antique store, same busy window filled with furniture and the case of knickknacks.

"What's the signal? Anyone?"

"Bottom shelf, right side. The vase is different."

"Is it?" Chin put up the original foil.

"Nope. Same vase," a different trainee declared. He blatted the sound of a "wrong answer" buzzer, and the class laughed.

But Laynie had spotted the signal; she'd seen it because she hadn't focused only on the window. She nodded to herself.

Chin replaced the original foil with the second one again. "Anyone have it? Anyone?" Chin looked at Laynie, and she smiled.

"You have it—right, Magda?"

"Yes."

The remainder of the class looked from her back to the second foil. After a moment, several said, "Got it," while others struggled to see what they'd missed.

"Magda, show them."

Laynie got up, walked to the projected image and pointed—not at the shop window, but at the wall that ran from the shop's corner down the building's side to a water spigot on the wall. "This."

Her finger touched the projection of a faint chalk mark next to the spigot. The mark was not more than an inch or two long.

Exclamations of surprised or muttered curses went around the classroom.

"Way to go, Maggie," Black said, giving credit where it was due.

"It was what you said—'It's like a signals smorgasbord'—that changed my focus, Black."

"Chuck," he muttered.

"'Fraid you're stuck with Black," Taylor laughed. "That's all Maggie calls you, so I think most of us think of you as Black, too." He added with a grin, "But, Black is better than Dudley . . . or *Dud*, right?"

He and Stephanie high-fived while Black growled, "Payback, buddy, payback. It's a-comin'."

Chin turned off the projector. "Groups of five. I want each group to devise a dead drop and a set of signals and be ready to demonstrate them tomorrow."

He pulled a box across his desk, opened it, and tossed decks of cards onto the desk. "These are your intel packets, and these are the rules: Drops and signals must be within the boundaries of the training grounds and in plain sight. You may utilize the public areas of the hotel, dining hall, and gym, and the external areas of the commissary and staff offices. Hide your packets, make your signals."

He pulled six Polaroid cameras from the box and plopped them on his desk. "Each group takes a camera. Come to class tomorrow with two photographs: The drop with the intel package inside and the posted signal. Be prepared to share your burn and danger signals, too.

"A last word: This is not a competition; it's a learning experience. Devise and justify. Poke holes in what doesn't work. Got it?"

Nora, Taylor, Black, Steph, and Laynie automatically formed a group, as did the other trainees with their dining partners. Nora retrieved a camera and an "intel packet."

"This should be fun," she grinned.

"Finding the time will be the issue," Laynie said. "We have our lunch period, the hour before dinner, and whatever time remains after dinner and the AAR."

"Let's brainstorm during lunch," Steph suggested.

WHEN CHIN DISMISSED them, they had fifteen minutes to use the restrooms, dress out for the gym, and report to their next class, which had four instructors—two men, two women.

"I'm Pelton; this is Lonetree, Montes, and Tillman. We're your hand-to-hand instructors." He moved to the center of the gym floor and Lonetree followed him. "Make a circle around me, please."

The trainees complied.

"Hand-to-hand is close-quarters battle with one or more adversaries. It connotes fighting for your freedom or your life. We don't train to a code or a style; we don't bow and show each other respect. We train you to survive, to win. To win, you may need to use whatever weapons you have on you and around you, and that means no available weapon is off limits. However, you are limited by how skilled you are with those weapons.

"We'll start with our bodies as our weapons. Every part of our body can damage an enemy, even kill him: Take the human hand. With it, you can punch with a fist, slice with the side of your palm, gouge with your fingers. Knowing where to deliver the blow is as essential as how to deliver it."

Lonetree stood passively while Pelton—with no weight behind any of his moves--demonstrated. His fist jumped out and connected (barely) with Lonetree's Adam's apple. "A blow to the throat can stun, paralyze, or kill."

Lonetree balled his fists and struck back. As he did, Pelton ducked under Lonetree's extended arm, moving around him. Pelton opened his hand and, with stiffened fingers, jabbed into Lonetree's open and vulnerable armpit.

"Youch," someone muttered.

As Lonetree recoiled, Pelton whirled and sliced the back and side of his opponent's waistline. Lonetree went to his knees.

"Excruciating nerve pain under the arm followed by blows to the kidney," Pelton pronounced, "using only my fist, my fingers, and the side of my hand.

"Now, I'm going to turn you over to Montes and Tillman who will work with you to optimize the three uses of your hands as weapons—fists, sides, and fingers. Then you'll practice on our dummies over there."

"Over there" was the end of the gym where three rubbery dummies on weighted stands stood ready for them.

Tillman and Montes described and demonstrated ten different attack moves, while explaining that a female agent had to employ any and every advantage to offset a male's physical advantages in height, weight, reach, and strength.

Eventually, the class lined up in three groups to deliver to the dummies the blows Tillman and Montes had demonstrated.

At Tillman's shouted commands, Laynie gouged the dummy's eyes with her fingers, throat-punched him, and kidney-sliced him. Over and over. She used the flat of her hands to clap the dummy's ears simultaneously, a move Tillman promised would remove a man's hands from around a woman's throat. "If you're being choked, don't go for the hands choking you—this is wasted, futile effort. Go for the eyes, ears, throat, and nuts."

When ordered, Laynie was to punch the dummy in his "family jewels"—a cheap shot, Montes screamed at Laynie, that would save her life someday.

Laynie, fueled by Montes' shouted intensity, drove her fist into the specified target, imagining how a male attacker would outweigh her, have a longer reach, and own the stronger blows.

After their second shower of the day, the trainees dressed and dragged themselves to the dining hall. Laynie should have been exhausted, but she'd left the class keyed up with adrenaline and the desire to learn more. She fidgeted over her lunch and found it hard to concentrate on their dead drop exercise.

"Dang, Mags," Taylor said. "I was watching you attack that dummy, and you really got into it. I daresay that dummy won't be fathering any kids after you finished with him."

Laynie finally relaxed. "Got my blood up, I guess."

"Well, just don't do that to me when we get to sparring, okay?" Taylor ribbed her.

Black pulled them on task. "C'mon; let's get to our dead drop exercise, okay? Any ideas?"

THE NEXT MORNING, the six groups presented their dead-drop exercises to the class. Chin had the other groups critique each presentation. They spent an hour picking apart the ambiguities, drawbacks, or issues they noted.

Three of the groups had used the dining hall's bulletin board for signals; one group had left a wad of gum on the base of the flagpole. Laynie and her team turned a flowerpot so that the red geranium (as opposed to the pink one) faced outward. For their danger signal, they cut off the red blooms. To signal that the op was "burned," they were much more dramatic: They pulled the plant out of the pot.

"I hate you guys," Lesley, a female trainee remarked. "Uprooting flowers is wrong!"

Her comment elicited chuckles from the class, but an unfortunate group earned derision instead. They had placed chalk marks on the tires of a staff vehicle that was regularly parked outside the staff offices.

Black shook his head at their mistake. “Do you control that vehicle? Just because it’s usually there doesn’t mean it couldn’t be driven off at any time, right? What then?”

“Good,” Chin said. “You’re getting the hang of the process, what works and what doesn’t. Remember, when you are charged in the future with running an op, it will be up to you to devise clever, foolproof means of communication.

SATURDAY EVENING finally arrived, and the trainees gathered in the dining hall for dinner. Laynie got her tray, filled it, and settled into her seat with Black, Steph, Nora, and Taylor. She picked up her fork and then paused. Set it down. Looked around their table.

“What?” Steph asked.

“I’m pausing to reflect, to make a memory,” Laynie said. “Stop with me for just a minute.”

She laid her palms flat on the table and waited. The others, after a moment, followed suit.

“What memory, Maggie?” Black teased. “Like, how many bruises you have from landing on your butt seventeen times this week?”

Taylor guffawed. “Pretty sure that was seventeen times every *day* this week, bro.”

“Give it a rest, you stupid, witless blokes.” Nora wasn’t putting up with the guys’ banter at present. “Maggie’s trying to say something serious to us. Go on, now. Tell us what you mean.”

Laynie tipped a half-smile in Nora’s direction. “I guess what I mean is this: Think back to last Sunday afternoon, the day we arrived here, a week ago tomorrow. Consider what’s happened since then, in six short days. What we’ve seen, what we’ve learned, what we’ve done, what we’ve fought through.

“Like, what we didn’t know about tradecraft then versus what we know now. What we didn’t know about firearms then; what we know now. What we hadn’t experienced before this week, and how these past six days have already changed us, dramatically, from who and what we were, to who and what we are becoming. Compare yourself now to that person last Sunday afternoon.

“Do you see? This week is the pivot point in our lives. None of us will ever again be who we were last Sunday due to this experience. I just thought it was worthwhile making note of it before it passes because . . .

because the *who* I will be at the end of this course? Well, I'm excited—and a little anxious, if I'm being frank—to meet that person."

She exhaled and picked up her fork. "I guess what I'm saying is, whatever it costs me, I'm in this thing."

"Hear, hear," Nora agreed, lifting her water glass. "Whatever the cost, we're in it!"

Laynie put down her fork and lifted her glass. They all did.

The five of them clinked their glasses and vowed with one voice, "Whatever the cost!"

Chapter 7

THE TRAINEES WERE hard into the second full week of the program. By now, they had the daily schedule planted in their minds: PT before breakfast, tradecraft after breakfast; hand-to-hand training for an hour and a half before lunch, firearms training for two hours after lunch; team obstacle course work for an hour, followed by showers yet again; more tradecraft consisting of case studies and films from 4 to 5 p.m.; an hour's break before dinner and, finally, the daily after action review—in which the mistakes any trainee may have made were dissected and remedies discussed.

Laynie and her classmates had grown accustomed to the firing range and its norms, to the mandatory rangewear and eye and ear protection, to promptly obeying instructions. The six firearms instructors, under the oversight of Mr. Henry, the rangemaster, had drilled the trainees on the rules of firearms safety until the students could repeat—and follow them—in their sleep.

On their second day on the range, the instructors had placed a series of handguns in the trainees' hands, beginning with a Smith & Wesson Model 10 snubnose revolver. The trainees practiced thumbing open the cylinder, dropping the six .38 Special rounds into the cylinder, and reloading until they could do it flawlessly in under ten seconds. When they had mastered manual loading, they were given speedloaders, a preloaded cylindrical device that allowed them to drop all six rounds into the revolver's cylinder at once, cutting the loading speed in half and reducing the likelihood of fumbling and dropping bullets—an essential consideration in a firefight.

"You won't always have speedloaders; someday your life may depend upon your facility to load manually, to do so quickly and without dropping bullets," Mr. Benelli told them. "This is why we train you to excel at both."

After that, Mr. de Guerre demonstrated a two-handed grip and the isosceles stance, where the shooter faced the target squarely, feet shoulder-width apart, knees somewhat bent, arms extended straight out before him, forming the isosceles triangle. Using unloaded revolvers, the trainees practiced the demonstrated stance, aiming their guns down range.

Then they loaded and shot the revolvers at targets a mere three yards away. The six instructors moved from student to student, correcting stances, adjusting grips, and loosening elbows to absorb recoil.

"Do not allow the muzzle of your firearm to rise or 'pop up' in an uncontrolled manner as you fire. Control your firearm; do not let it control you. A strong, firm grip will limit the rise and will help keep the barrel level with the target so that successive shots remain on target."

Then, with a stopwatch running, the trainees dropped their expended shells, manually reloaded, shot, dropped the shells, reloaded, and shot again—repeating the exercise until they could fire and reload twice in under ten seconds, flawlessly. When the students completed an exercise, they laid their revolvers on the bench in front of them—cylinder open and empty, barrel pointing down range—and faced away from the range to await their next set of instructions.

Between drills, one of the range staff, a woman named Steyr, shouted, "Trainees! What you must understand is that weapons handling and marksmanship are perishable skills, meaning they have a short shelf life. This maxim applies to handguns in particular! We will review the fundamentals and practice them, *ad infinitum*, because your success in the field proceeds from those fundamentals."

A second instructor, Weatherby, added, "Our focus at this moment is not on your marksmanship but on your intimate familiarity with your weapon's weight, feel, and workings. Precision loading and unloading—doing so quickly, without fumbling—are essential components to surviving a real firefight. Why? Because when your life is on the line, your gun must be an extension of your hand: Loading and unloading it must be an automatic, unconscious act. When you are so familiar with your weapon's workings that muscle memory takes over, you can then focus all of your attention on your target and your situation.

"Remember, the best you can do in a firefight is limited by the training and equipment you bring to that fight. Training, therefore, is as important as the weapon you carry."

Steyr took over. "Furthermore, as a covert operative in the field, you will not carry a firearm openly as law enforcement officers do. In fact, many theaters of operation forbid civilian carry and/or ownership of firearms. For this reason, you will handle and shoot a variety of handguns to broaden your experience, including several models that are smaller and easier to conceal than a full-sized gun."

Under the instructors' watchful eyes, the trainees cleaned and oiled their revolvers. The two armorers then collected the revolvers and issued semiautomatic handguns and magazines in their place.

The issued Beretta 92 was a more complex mechanism than the revolver, but it had certain advantages over a revolver: The Beretta shot fifteen 9mm rounds from a double-stack magazine opposed to the revolver's six rounds, and a fully loaded magazine could replace an empty one in half the time it took to manually reload a six-shot revolver.

Before the trainees picked up the Beretta, Weatherby spoke to them. "Listen up! Even after you have dropped the magazine, a semiauto can have a round already chambered. You are to visually inspect the magazine well *and* the chamber. *Look* to verify that the magazine has been ejected and that no cartridge is chambered. *Use your index finger* to check for a round in the chamber. You must check both the magazine well and the chamber before declaring that your weapon is cleared."

The instructors walked the trainees through loading and unloading their magazines, seating the magazines in the handgun, pulling back the slide to chamber a round—then removing the magazine, locking back the slide (ejecting the chambered round), and visually and physically inspecting the magazine well and chamber to ensure that they were both empty.

Laynie performed the drill until the Beretta in her hand felt natural and the steps to load and unload as common as tying her shoes. Stripping and cleaning the weapon took longer to learn but that process, too, soon became second nature. Shooting the semiauto was also easier than shooting the double-action revolver, and the slide locked back, telling you when the magazine was empty.

Once the trainees were familiar with both revolver and semiauto handguns, the instructors worked on their marksmanship. Some students (Black for one) were proficient shots, while Laynie, always competitive, felt that she merely muddled along, making small but noticeable improvements day by day.

When the armorers had collected the handguns and Mr. Henry, the rangemaster, had issued the "all clear," the instructors lowered the red flag at the back corner of the range that denoted active shooting. After that, the students policed their shooting stations, pulling on gloves, collecting the spent brass, and dumping the casings into a receptacle nearby.

While Laynie picked up spent casings she thought, *I might become a marginally capable shot someday—at close range—but I doubt I'll be better than that. Then again, will I ever need to use a handgun except in an emergency situation?*

During her musings, it dawned on Laynie that her competence in any given "emergency situation" would likely mean the difference between life and death.

Her death.

Shaking her head, Laynie ordered herself to redouble her efforts to achieve more than a "passing" competence.

THE NEXT FOUR WEEKS passed in a flurry of unrelenting work, and the trainees (down from thirty to twenty-five) were gaining confidence in their skills.

In tradecraft they'd become proficient at brush passes, dead drops, live drops, surveillance detection and evasion, and covert surveillance of others. They'd learned and utilized differing communication methodologies: shortwave and two-way radio, Morse code, signal flags, simple codes and codebreaking. They could pick locks and pockets, duplicate keys and IDs, hotwire cars and trucks. And they'd watched countless reels of training films, learning to spot the moves that appeared on the screen (from top-tier performances, through amateur, down to the bottom—the demonstrably awful). They'd picked apart what worked and what didn't, learned to emulate what was effective and to shun poor tradecraft. They came to value an adept performance and deride their own mistakes.

In hand-to-hand combat, the trainees grappled with experienced fighters whose frequent "schoolings" sent trainees crashing to the mats time and again . . . until the trainees put their heart into the fight, determined to give as good as they got.

Then the trainees tackled each other—and they burned with fierce competition.

Although trainees wore padded headgear and mouthguards, bruises (on pretty much any part of the body) were common and no longer remarked upon.

Their instructors advanced them into the use of weapons during hand-to-hand starting with a variety of saps, sticks, and expandable batons. They taught the students how to make a weapon from whatever furniture or articles were around them. In an outdoor arena at the back of the gym, the trainees practiced destroying melons, boards, flowerpots, chairs, and other targets—the men especially enthusiastic participants in these exercises—and how to use whatever came to hand to attack dummies identified as enemy opponents.

The instructors taught the trainees how to handle knives of all lengths—straight, folding, switchblades, serrated, stilettos—and anything with a pointy end or a slicing edge able to penetrate human skin. They issued hard rubber knives, and the trainees practiced with them against experienced fighters less likely to wound them or be wounded. Three trainees still managed to require stitches during those skirmishes.

The trainees learned, too, how diabolically devious Gunny's assistants were at changing up the obstacle courses. Unexpected variations, additions, and deletions to the courses forced the teams to think collectively and outside the box, work as a cohesive unit, and lean upon each other's strengths. As week succeeded week, the teams had to move faster and solve problems quicker to complete a course at or under the set time, developing almost hive-like communication skills in the process.

As their sixth week on the firing range came to a close, the trainees regularly shot a variety of handguns, bolt-action rifles, semiauto rifles (including the M1 Carbine, a WWII standard phased out during the Vietnam war but still in wide circulation across Europe, the ArmaLite AR-10, Springfield Armory's M1A, and several rifles built on the ArmaLite AR-15 design), and shotguns of varying lengths and gauges.

Laynie's first-choice weapon for accuracy was the Heckler & Koch HK43 semiauto rifle with its collapsible stock that fit her body well. She also liked the M6 Scout by Springfield Armory and the Steyr AUG assault rifle—but her favorite was the Mossberg 500 shotgun. It was short, easy to clean and maintain, and deadly in close-quarters.

Too bad I can't carry it up my skirt, right?

She snickered to herself. *Yes, the Mossberg is effective, but it's also about as subtle as a root canal.*

IT WAS DURING that sixth week on the range, while cleaning their weapons, that Black smacked his forehead with the palm of his hand.

"Okay, call me dense, but I've just figured something out. I mean, wow. Can't believe how dense I am."

"Whereas *we* have no difficulty believing," Stephanie, on the other side of Black, tossed back with her pixie grin.

Black hung his head. "You wound me, Steph."

Laynie, at the next station over, was preoccupied with stripping down the compact, semiauto Walther she'd just fired. "What? What are you blathering on about?"

"At last! Someone who listens!" He turned to Laynie. "You know the training staff? All the instructors? Even the armorers? Just like our names are aliases, their names are too."

Laynie looked up from her task. "So?"

"Yeah. So?" Steph mocked.

"So, they've been pretty inventive with their names. In fact, I'm thinking they took some pleasure in constructing their faux identities."

Now he had their attention. Laynie demanded, "Do tell."

"I don't know why it didn't hit sooner. The range staff? Just list off their names. There's Benelli, Walther, de Guerre, Weatherby, Mossberg, and Springfield—those names are all firearms manufacturers. Moreover, Benelli is an *Italian* manufacturer, Walther is *German*, and de Guerre is *Belgian*.

"What? Are you saying the instructors' names somehow match their nationalities?"

"We're not supposed to delve into trainee or instructor backgrounds, remember? 'Aliases equal anonymity,' so I'll just leave it right there. But then there's our illustrious rangemaster, Mr. *Henry*, which only furthers my case."

Laynie laughed out loud. "This is great. What else have the staff put over on us?"

"Well, that's where they got all cutesy with their aliases. Vickers? Olifant and Stridsvagn? Do you get it?"

Stephanie looked confused; Laynie shook her head. "Nope. Outside my wheelhouse, I guess."

"They're tanks."

"What are tanks?"

"Their names! Their names are tanks."

"Tanks? You mean, like, army tanks?"

"Yes; their names are all tank models and manufacturers. Furthermore, Vickers is a *British* tank and Stridsvagn is a *Swedish* tank. Again, I'm not digging into their nationalities; just putting it out there."

"I think you're on to something, Black."

"What about Chin?" Steph asked. "Is he a tank?"

Black laughed. "Nope. Better. His moniker is that of an *infamous spy*, and he's not the only one on campus. So are Pelton, Lonetree, Montes, and Tillman. So, can you visualize it? Our stuffy, uptight senior staff and instructors getting together to plan their jokey little aliases?"

Laynie chucked. "Oh, yeah, I can see it now: An evening of pizza, beer, and laughing up their sleeves."

Steph snickered. "Huh. Not as stuffy as they put on; not as tough and lacking in a sense of humor as they'd like us to believe, are they?"

"Except Trammel. Haven't caught on to his alias yet."

Laynie shook her head. "Sorry. I can't see him choosing a tank or an infamous spy for his moniker."

Steph agreed. "Nope. He's too scary. No pizza, beer, and yukking it up for him."

THE TRAINEES, numbering twenty, gutted out a seventh week. Saturday evening at dinner, having reached the midpoint of their training, the staff rewarded the trainees with ice cream sundaes.

Laynie, Black, Steph, Nora, and Taylor grabbed two paper cups apiece, filled them with ice cream and drenched the ice cream in sugary sauces and toppings to celebrate their accomplishments.

"Don't know about you guys," Steph said, scraping the bottom of her second sundae, "but I'm looking forward to our half-day off tomorrow and a nice, long nap."

Nora nodded with vigor. "I'll be honest with you blokes: I've never been so absolutely quanked in my life. I'd love nothing more than to sleep all afternoon—but I need to do my washing up."

Taylor, sprawled in his chair as usual, with an assiduously straight face focused on his last bite, muttered, "I *thought* I smelled something ripe. Wait—was that coming from you?"

When Black, Steph, and Laynie howled with laughter, Nora socked Taylor in the arm.

"You're a beast, Tay. A perfectly *awful* beast."

Taylor leaned toward her making puppy-dog eyes. "Ah, Nora, my sweet! You do mean I'm a *lovable* beast, don't you?"

"No, you're *awful*, Tay. Perfectly awful!"

"Thank you for confirming, in public, that I'm perfect."

The others roundly pelted him with crumpled paper cups and napkins.

AT THE CONCLUSION of dinner, Trammel stood to address the trainees. "In recognition of your hard work up to this midpoint in your training, we will forego this evening's AAR. However, I have an announcement to make.

"Monday morning, you will begin a period of immersive SERE training—Marstead style. SERE stands for Survival, Evasion, Resistance, and Escape. No, we won't be doing every aspect of SERE training but, for this iteration, you will be bussed to a different facility, one with which you have no familiarity.

"Listen up! The hardships and challenges you have experienced and overcome during the past seven weeks are a mere walk in the park compared to what's coming. The best preparation—the only preparation—for SERE is this: Be ready to surmount anything. That is all. Have a good evening."

"*Have a good evening*, he says," Nora groused. "Bloody ruined it for us, he did."

CHAPTER 8

LP

SUNDAY MORNING BEGAN like any other morning: PT, followed by breakfast, tradecraft, and hand-to-hand. After lunch, however, the trainees were on their own to rest and recuperate. Laynie, like most of the trainees, used the afternoon to catch up on personal chores—laundry, mending, and a quick phone call home.

Two rooms on the hotel's first floor were set apart for phone calls. The rooms were soundproofed and equipped with special phones and doors that locked. Trainees signed up for fifteen-minute slots on the room's door.

Laynie locked the door behind her and picked up the phone. A Marstead operator put her call through—and a look at a dump of those phones' records would show that the calls came from Marstead's D.C. offices, not a compound in the mountains of Virginia.

"Mama? Hi, it's Laynie."

"Laynie-girl!"

"How are you and Dad? Tell me about your trip up to Vancouver? What does Sammie say about his new semester, Mama?"

Laynie came prepared with questions because of the little she could say about her own activities. Although she missed her family and loved to hear their voices, she had also come to appreciate the wisdom of a fifteen-minute limit to calls home.

"My classmates are starting a volleyball game soon, Mama. I promised to play, and I need to put my wet laundry in the dryer before we start. All right. I love you too, Mama. Miss you all. Talk to you next week. Bye."

The little lies seemed to come so easily.

SHE DIDN'T TAKE PART in the referenced volleyball game until after dinner, but even then, she dropped out early, intent on logging a few extra hours of sleep before the SERE course began Monday morning.

She'd been asleep less than four hours when, at 12:01 a.m., the new week officially arrived. Laynie sat up in bed, shaken awake by the thundering of heavy boots in the hall, to fists pounding on doors and shouted commands.

She understood at once what was happening. *They've pulled a fast one on us.*

Grateful for a dresser filled with clean clothes and for the long-sleeved shirt she'd donned before bed, Laynie grabbed a pair of camo trousers and yanked them on as fast as she could.

Boots! Socks and boots!

She didn't move fast enough. She had one sock on, when her door burst open.

"Get her!"

Two men, features concealed by ski masks to hide their identities, rushed her. Laynie had enough time to grab her boots before the men were on her. She folded her arms across her boots and did not let go, even when they yanked her to her feet, threw a black cloth bag over her head, and herded her into the hall.

As they traversed the hotel's second floor, Laynie heard a woman's scream of protest.

Laynie ground her teeth. *Note to self: Don't sleep naked the night before SERE training.*

Her captors rushed her down to ground level.

Blind, but aware of how important her boots would be in the coming week, Laynie clung to them, even as unseen hands pushed and pulled at her and shouted orders to her and her classmates. She was shoved into other bodies, bodies that stepped on her unprotected toes, and she could feel the warmth of those bodies, hear their panting, heavy breathing, an occasional muttered word, and one or two moans of pain.

Evidently, a few of her fellow trainees had resisted and had paid for it.

These instructors aren't messing around.

Laynie slid her boots under her t-shirt and wrapped her arms around her middle to secure them. She didn't want to think about being stuck barefoot for a week; it was bad enough she hadn't had time to snatch up the other sock. The impression of a raw, blistered foot rose before her.

Someone grabbed her hands; Laynie kept her forearms and elbows pinned across her boots as a nylon noose encircled her wrists, tightened, and someone tied it off.

"Get on the bus! Get on the bus!" their captors screamed.

They were herded forward. Some bright trainee, stumbling at the bus steps, hollered, "Steps!" Laynie gauged the distance to his voice as best she could in her sightless state and slid in behind a male body, intending to use him as her "step detector."

As she'd expected, the trainee, unable to see the steps, rammed his shins into them. He cursed and stumbled upward. Laynie was ready and managed to navigate the steps without too much difficulty—until a hand pushed her from behind and she fell in the stair well. She struggled to her feet, climbed up, and started down the aisle; then another hand thrust her into a seat.

"Move over! Move to the window!"

Laynie got over into the window seat seconds before another body plunked into the seat she'd vacated. She leaned toward the body. Whispered.

"I'm Maggie. Who are you?"

The whispered answer came back, "Brett."

She knew Brett; he was an okay guy. "We'll get through this."

"You telling me? Or yourself?"

"Both of us."

A captor screamed, "Shut up! No talking!"

Laynie whispered anyway, "We should sleep; we're going to need it." She took her own advice, leaned against the window, and willed herself to sleep.

LATER, THE BUS TURNED off the paved road and bumped over rugged terrain. Laynie woke, her neck stiff, the boots gouging her sides. She thought it must still be dark outside. They were offloaded into a building, a room.

The doors banged shut behind them.

"Listen up! My men will be going around to remove your restraints and the bags over your heads. As soon as they have, you are to sit down where you are."

It took about five minutes for their captors, faces still concealed, to cut their restraints and for the trainees to hunker down on the cold floor and wait for whatever came next. Laynie peered around, first to mark the location of the jailers in the room, then to locate Nora, Steph, Taylor, and Black. In addition to the ski masks, the instructors, just two of them, were dressed in ordinary dark street clothes.

The man who'd given the order for them to be released stood silent at the front of the room, waiting until he had their full attention. He did not hide his face; his expression was hard and callous, colder than any mask.

When the room settled, he spoke.

"My name is Rafe, and I run this course. I will remind you that you are not soldiers but private citizens. Therefore, unlike military versions of this course, we will not instill in you a military code of conduct. We will, instead, teach you how to protect your mission, your fellow operatives, and your network—at all costs, using all possible measures at your disposal.

"This SERE course differs in other ways from military courses, just as covert operatives differ from soldiers. As you will not be lawful combatants in a declared war, the rules of warfare and the Geneva Conventions would not apply to you in a real SERE situation. The enemy will know this and exploit it; you must know and accept it, too: *All rules are off the table*. Fix it in your minds now that you must survive, evade, resist, and escape though any means possible, without restriction—because the enemy will not be bound by restrictions either.

"A usual SERE course might offer the basics of outdoor survival such as woodcraft, how to build fires, purify water, improvise shelter, set snares, etc. As your theater of operation will normally be urban, we will forego fieldcraft; our evasion exercise will be conducted in an urban environment.

"You will learn interrogation resistance—how to survive and resist the enemy in the event of capture. You will learn how to withstand demands for information—to prevaricate, to deflect, and to provide disinformation.

"A word about interrogation in general: Because you will not be lawful combatants, if you are captured and interrogated, it is highly likely that your interrogation will include torture. This course will test your determination to protect your operation and network under adverse circumstances."

The quiet room grew quieter still.

"The course will work like this: You will pair up, ten teams of two. Each team will be given an intelligence package. You would do well to memorize that intelligence and then destroy it.

"Your team will be dropped in an urban location with a map to a safe destination and a ten-minute lead. Your task is to deliver the intelligence to your superiors at the destination on your map. You will be pursued by two armed operatives. Their task is to capture you and the intelligence package: You will *not* allow them to capture the package."

He held up a black, rectangular, palm-sized device. "You will each be issued a weapon. These are your weapons—stun guns. They do not fire projectiles; they require direct contact. If you stun a pursuer, he or she is considered dead and will break off pursuit and return to enemy HQ. If *you* are stunned, your pursuers will take you captive and convey you to their headquarters to extract the intelligence from you.

"For every team captured and conveyed to the enemy HQ, that team's pursuers are freed up to assist in the capture of teams still at large, meaning the last team at large may have a sizable number of pursuers after them. When you are captured—and you will be—you will be interrogated."

Rafe looked around. "Let me be clear: We are not your friends; we are here to provide a realistic experience. You may well hate us when this exercise is finished—which is why none of your instructors are participating. Any questions?"

A female trainee said, "Since we were yanked from our beds, some of us are without proper clothing, especially shoes. What—"

"I suggest you improvise—as you would in the field."

"What about the police?" a trainee asked. "What if they see us and think our behavior is suspicious?"

"The police have been notified that a military SERE exercise is in process. If they pull you aside, you are to ask, 'Do you know Engelbert Humperdinck's song, *Release Me?*'"

Normally, that corny line would have generated a spate of groans. Not today. The trainees took in the information without comment.

Amid the silence that followed, someone dared to ask, "Sir, what is the duration of this exercise? When is it over?"

Rafe's chuckle was laden with unpleasant, hidden meaning—and the hair on Laynie's arms prickled and stood up. "The exercise is over when all teams have been captured and interrogated."

A number of curses floated through the trainee group.

"Get up," Rafe ordered. "Choose your teammates now. You will draw your weapons, maps, intel packages, and ten dollars in cash in the next room and be taken, team by team, to a drop-off location. Your pursuers are already in place. As you are dropped off, your driver will radio your pursuers and your ten-minute lead will commence."

Laynie jumped to her feet with the other trainees. She wanted to pair up with Black; instead, Taylor grabbed her arm.

"Team up with me, Mags," he whispered. "We can do this."

She nodded. "Agreed."

In the next room, the teams collected their intel packages, maps, cash, and stun guns. Black and Stephanie had paired up; Nora was with another female trainee. They nodded a sober and silent "good luck" to each other, then gave themselves to the tasks at hand.

The drop-offs were staggered, three vans, one team to a van, taking about forty-five minutes to deploy each team. That gave the waiting teams time to strategize. Laynie and Taylor were no different. They examined their stun guns, familiarizing themselves with their action. They read and memorized their intel packets and studied their maps.

Laynie put on her boots—one foot minus a sock. Taylor was barefoot, clad in only a t-shirt and shorts.

"More than one person got caught sleeping naked. They let them cover themselves with the minimum, but no footwear. How did you manage to get your boots?"

"Heard the guys coming; threw on my pants, grabbed the boots, and held on for dear life."

"I need shoes. We'll have to hit a store as soon as we find one that's open."

"Won't our pursuers know the location of every store near our drop-off?"

"Ah. Good point."

WHEN LAYNIE AND Taylor's drop time came, they climbed into a van and were blindfolded. The van then drove for about twenty minutes. During the drive, Taylor shed his t-shirt and tore it into strips and pieces that he tied on his feet. When the van stopped, the driver pulled off their blindfolds and said, "Get out. The ten-minute clock starts in five seconds."

Laynie and Taylor had already strategized. They took a few seconds to scan their surroundings before picking a direction. Their first thought had been to run. It didn't matter in which direction, really: Distance from the drop point was what counted.

But, while planning, they'd reconsidered.

From what they saw around them, they figured themselves to be somewhere north of D.C.—and not anywhere upscale, either. The storefronts around them were ill-kept and rundown, many closed; trash had piled up in the gutters; and the only person on the street this early in the morning stared at them with thinly veiled hostility.

"Let's get away from prying eyes," Taylor suggested.

They crossed the street, ran two blocks, took a left at the next intersection, ran half a block, then ducked between two buildings. The length of the "between" contained two dumpsters overflowing with garbage. The "between" also had doors leading into the adjacent buildings—but they were both solid and locked tight. The long alleyway also dead-ended at a high, discolored cyclone fence topped with nasty-looking, rusted barbed wire.

"That there is a tetanus convention just waiting for roll call," Taylor muttered.

They peered out from between the buildings, scouring the street. Two cars were parked along their side of the street; a rusty pickup sat across the street, several yards farther from the intersection at which they'd turned.

"I think this is as good a place as any we'll find." Laynie pointed to the two cars parked along the curb a few feet away. She indicated the vehicle that had a flat tire, the driver's window cracked and crazed. "That one."

Taylor picked up a rock, hammered a fist-sized hole through the cracked glass, reached in, and unlocked the door. Laynie handed Taylor her stun gun and scooted behind the wheel, then over to the passenger seat. She stared up the street, to the intersection where they'd turned.

"Five or six minutes gone, you think?"

"Sounds about right. Another five before they come after us, not more than five minutes more before they sweep this street."

Laynie took a deep breath. "Yeah. Ten minutes total, give or take. Okay. Good luck, Tay."

"You, too, Mags."

Taylor strode between the buildings and stationed himself at the corner of the wall where he could watch for the pursuers.

Ten minutes passed, then five more, before they heard the slow idle of a muscle car approaching. They exchanged glances and nodded. Taylor ducked back into the short "alley"; Laynie stretched herself out on the car's musty front seat.

She listened closely, focusing on the car's growling engine. It paused in the intersection. A car door opened and closed quietly, before the car turned left and cruised slowly toward them.

Laynie waited until the car had passed; she had to time it "just right" before she showed herself. She counted to ten, gauging how far down the street the car was, how close she believed the pursuer who'd gotten out would be.

She sat up, head turned, staring after the car. She immediately opened the passenger door and crept out.

A shout and the pounding of boots signaled that the on-foot pursuer had seen her. With a glance over her shoulder, she jetted in the direction of the passing pursuit car—but the driver had heard his partner. Tires squealed as he stomped the brakes; the driver threw the transmission into park, jumped out, and headed for Laynie.

With pursuers ahead and behind, Laynie shot across the street and up the sidewalk. She rounded the rusted-out truck at the curb, but her pursuers had flanked her again and were closing in. Laynie vaulted onto the hood of the truck, tumbled over it, and again headed across the street, this time aiming for the "alley" between the two buildings. She slid between the parked cars and, putting on a burst of speed, raced down the alley between the buildings—only to fly up against the cyclone fence. She whirled, thinking to return to the sidewalk before her pursuers arrived, but when she turned, they already stood at the top of the alley.

Laynie was trapped. She turned and began a mad scramble up the rusted fencing.

"Won't do you any good, missy. See that barbed wire up there? You're not getting over that."

Laynie, about five feet off the ground, stared up at the top of the fence.

That there is a tetanus convention just waiting for roll call.

Clinging to the fence and edging higher, she began to shriek. Her panicked screams, echoing between the high brick buildings, were terrifying even to her—and loud enough to raise the dead.

"Stick her, Dirk! Shut her the **blank** up!"

Metal jabbed the back of Laynie's leg, and her calf muscle became the entry point for a bolt of pure pain. Her screams fused to her throat; every muscle in her body spasmed and locked up. When they unlocked seconds later, her fingers were lifeless. She fell backward, off the fence.

Her pursuers caught and flipped her over in one move and expertly pinned her, pressing her face into the alley's filth. One grabbed Laynie's wrists; the other pulled flex cuffs from his belt.

"Her partner has to be close by," he said.

"Actually, I'm right here, dirtbags."

As he spoke, Taylor, a stun gun in each hand, stuck the men and depressed both buttons at once. Their pursuers convulsed, moaned, thrashed, and collapsed.

Taylor helped Laynie to her feet. She was shaking, but recovering.

"Nice diversion, Mags."

"Thanks, Tay."

Taylor turned to the two men sprawled on their faces. "Well, since you guys are both dead, guess you won't be needing your car."

"H-hey, no. You can't do that."

"Rafe said, 'All rules are off the table.' Just playin' it like he said." Taylor sketched a laughing salute. "See ya 'round, chumps!"

He dragged Laynie from the alley to the car idling in the street, and they drove off.

"G-good job, Tay."

"You, too, Mags. Sorry they zapped you."

"No matter. Listen, if we've got the intel packet memorized, let's dump it now."

"*If* we have it memorized?"

"I know; I had it down at age two and you probably did, too, but we can't be caught with the package."

Taylor pulled over to a gutter grate. Laynie opened her door and tossed the package down the grate.

"Okay, that's done. Now, let's get to our safe house."

Their map, which they had also studied and committed to memory, had only a single reference somewhere near the drop-off location and a compass to indicate the map's orientation. It listed no street names or other markers, only a street grid with their destination marked by the initials, "TT." Ordinarily, in order for the map to make sense, they would have had to find the starting reference point and work their way from there to their destination.

Instead, they drove due north until they spotted a gas station. Taylor pulled in; Laynie jumped out, taking the map and Taylor's ten bucks with her.

"Hi there," she smiled to the clerk. "Do you have any maps of this area?"

"Sure, the regular D.C. city and outlying areas maps."

"Well, my friend and I are on this treasure hunt of sorts—I know, fun, right? We're having a blast so far."

The clerk, looking barely out of high school, got excited. "Really? That's cool. You need any help?"

"We sure do. Thanks for offering. See, here's the map we've been given. Other than our destination, indicated as TT, the map has no street names or identifying landmarks, just this one building with the initials BSL. We need to know what and where BSL is so that the map will make sense and we can find our way to the treasure."

He frowned as he thought. "Suppose it could be Barrett Savings and Loan. Does that sound right?"

"Could you show me on a city map where it is?"

He pulled a city map from the rack and unfolded it. "Look. We're here. Barrett Savings and Loans is down Georgia Avenue, couple miles south."

Laynie turned her map to orient it to the city map. "You might be right. Could I borrow a pen?"

"Yup. Here."

She wrote "Georgia Avenue" in the margin of her map and drew a line to the street alongside their reference point, which she then labeled "Barrett Savings and Loan." From there, comparing her map to the city map, she slowly found her way to the intersection of 4th Street NW and Butternut Street NW. She placed her finger there.

"I'm looking for a building with the initials TT at this intersection. Any ideas?"

He pulled the map closer to him, made funny noises in his throat while thinking, then said, "Oh! I've got it. It's Takoma Theatre. Has to be. It's old. Used to be a real theatre—you know, for plays? Kind of a shabby movie house now. I hope somebody buys it and fixes it up someday."

Laynie drew a line from "TT" to the margin and printed, "Takoma Theatre."

"You've been great, man. Thanks. Say, you have any t-shirts?"

"Just the usual tourist trash."

Laynie walked back to the waiting car and slid inside. "Here. Got you a shirt. Hope you're a fan of George Washington University's Colonials. They're a basketball team."

"What's basketball?"

"Huh? Don't play much b-ball where you're from, huh?" She snickered, "No, forget it. Don't say a word. I know, *I know*: anonymity.

Anyway, I've identified our destination—it's an old movie house, Takoma Theatre. We can probably be there in half an hour if the traffic is decent."

"Way to go, Mags!"

TAYLOR PULLED THE car around to the back of the theater where the parking lot was. They got out. Two men saw them, exited their van, grinned and waved to them.

From yards away, one called, "Shoot—you guys are the first to hit your safe destination. Good job!" As they came up to Laynie and Taylor, the same guy squinted. "Wait—you hijacked Nelson and Dirk's ride? That's a first gen Camaro, man. Dirk's baby. Ballsy move, you two."

"You want us to drive it back?" Taylor asked.

"Naw, you can ride with us. We'll send someone for it—besides, I don't think you want to deliver it to Dirk in person. That would be like rubbing salt in the wound and, trust me, you don't want to do that."

Laynie had hung back a foot or so, but the second guy approached her, hand outstretched. "Congrats. It's Magda, right?"

"Call me Maggie," she said, shaking his hand.

That's when he hit her with the stun gun palmed in his other hand.

Laynie toppled like a pine in a hurricane.

"Whoa, little lady!" The man caught her and laid her down before she faceplanted on the pavement.

Seconds later, Taylor was twitching on the asphalt next to her.

In short order, the men had Laynie and Taylor in flex cuffs; two minutes after that, the men were marching/dragging them to the van. They pushed Laynie and Taylor into the back through the rear doors. There were no seats in the back; Laynie and Taylor fell awkwardly onto the van's floor, and Laynie caught her shin on something that stung her pretty good. The men then grabbed their ankles and flex cuffed them, too, before slamming the doors closed.

She recovered her voice before Taylor did. "You can't do this!" she croaked. "We won! We beat the exercise fair and square!"

"That's what they all say," the driver laughed. "They forget the part where Rafe says, 'The exercise is over when all teams have been captured and interrogated,' and my personal fav, 'When you are captured—and you will be—*you will be interrogated.*'"

Laynie squirmed around to face Taylor. "I can't believe we fell for it."

He didn't answer.

AFTERWARD, LAYNIE TRIED to remember the whole of the incarceration and interrogation, but the memories blurred in her mind or came back in horrid flashes of bits and pieces. She and Taylor were offloaded into a warehouse, tossed without ceremony, still cuffed, into a small, cold room. Laynie landed on her left elbow and hip.

Bruises upon bruises.

Then came the sprinklers, soaking them to the bone. Laynie managed to roll to a sitting position. She butt-walked to a wall, and leaned against it, but the wall was cold, too, and she was already shivering.

"B-back-to-back, Tay? M-might keep us warm."

They squirmed until their backs were together. It helped, a little—until the sprinklers came on again. Laynie sputtered and spit out water that dripped from her hairline into her eyes and mouth. With her hands bound behind her, she couldn't wipe her face.

Hours passed. Their jailers tossed other trainees into the cell—and followed up with more sprinklers and more soaking. The small room was soon crowded. Laynie counted sixteen trainees, Nora and her partner, too. Four to go, including Black and Stephanie.

Laynie's teeth chattered; she and Tay and others huddled to conserve warmth, but they were all stiff, cold, and crowded. Many were dispirited, and tempers flared; one trainee in particular, began shouting expletives and vile obscenities at their keepers . . . and then at Marstead. By name.

Taylor kicked him. Hard. "Shut up, man. These guys aren't *us*; get your head right. Remember your **bleeping** NDA and maintain proper OPSEC."

The doors opened. The last four trainees were shoved inside, only to fall over those closest to the doors. Steph moaned; Black might have been unconscious.

Then came the interrogations.

Two men in ski masks appeared at the doors holding clipboards. "Magda! Taylor!"

Armed with foot-long stun sticks, they waded through the crush of bodies, hauled Laynie and Taylor to their feet, and dragged them away.

Laynie heard someone shout, "Stay strong, Mags!"

Black.

What followed were hours—or maybe it was days?—of Laynie's arms lifted above her head, her flex cuffs caught on a hook in the ceiling, while she stood on a pile of concrete blocks—the pile not quite high enough to take the strain off her arms.

"Magda. Tell us about Mary. Tell us about Mary, and we'll let you go. C'mon, Magda."

Laynie kept her mouth shut—until her masked captors turned a high-pressure hose on her. The water beat her, stinging, pummeling, pounding, freezing.

"Tell us about Mary, Magda. Tell us what you know."

She shook her head.

It went on and on, the same questions, unrelenting pain in her shoulders, arms that she could no longer feel.

"Tell us about Mary and the guy with her! Tell us! Tell us where he went."

At some point, Laynie either slept or passed out. When they took her down, the blood flowed back into her arms in the shape of fiery needles. She screamed and moaned, then wept from the pain.

"Tell us about Mary, Magda. Who was with her? What color was his hair?"

Laynie sobbed once more and bit her lip to keep from moaning aloud. When she couldn't keep quiet, she cursed them.

"Okay, boys. Next step."

Three men grabbed her arms and legs and laid her on a plank, strapped her down, balanced the center of the plank on a chair. They lifted the plank and her feet, tipping her head toward a tin tub on the floor. Someone covered her face with a towel. Water poured through the towel, into her nose, her mouth. Then they tilted the plank upright and removed the towel.

Laynie couldn't catch her breath; she choked and coughed and spat water and phlegm.

"Tell us about Mary, Magda. Tell us about her little friend. What color was he, Magda? Where did he go?"

"I'll tell, I'll tell!" Laynie choked out.

"Good. That's good. Tell us, Magda, tell us all about Mary. One little verse, and this all stops. Just one. You can do that, can't you?"

Laynie grit her teeth and screamed. "Her name wasn't *Mary*, you **bleeping** idiots! Her name was BO PEEP, and she had a large, purple GOAT that found your shoes and ATE THEM!"

One of her captors at least had the decency to laugh, but the others cursed her—and recommenced her interrogation. She lost track of how many times they poured water through the towel onto her face.

When she had passed out twice, they dumped her in a corner for a while to work on someone else. When they started up on her again, Laynie didn't have the strength to keep coughing up water. When she quit, they yanked her to a sitting position while someone stood behind her and performed abdominal thrusts to bring up the fluids.

Laynie was semiconscious, in a dreamlike state.

Hey, I know that procedure—I'm a lifeguard. Who's drowning?

When she woke up, she was back in the holding tank. Around her, her fellow trainees were coughing and spitting; the room was rank with sweat and urine and vomit. More than one trainee wept, although they tried to keep it quiet.

Laynie leaned against someone—she didn't know or care who—and slept.

They came for her two more times, and she endured. She was only able to because, *I know what they will and won't do. I outlasted them once; I can do it again.*

And then Rafe stood in the doorway. His masked goons walked among the trainees' sprawled bodies, cutting flex cuffs.

"Course is over. Get on the bus."

LAYNIE WAS SO tired, she could barely move. Then she saw Black waiting for her, leaning heavily against the bus.

"C'mon, Mags. Sit with me."

"Okay."

They found seats together, and she pressed into his shoulder, wanting nothing more than to sleep. However, before the bus pulled out, two men, strangers as far as they knew, boarded the bus. They began handing out burgers, fries, and root beer.

"Ohhhh . . ." Laynie moaned, sinking her teeth into the hot burger.

CHAPTER 9

LP

IT WAS FRIDAY AFTERNOON when they returned to the Marstead compound. The doctors were on hand to check the trainees for injuries; they prescribed pain killers, muscle relaxers, and sleeping pills for whomever wanted them. They placed a finger splint on a trainee who'd resisted on his third water boarding. After medical exams, the class was down five trainees.

Laynie exhaled a long, resigned breath. *I'm surprised it isn't more.*

The doctors also prescribed a day of complete rest to include three hearty meals. That was Saturday.

The next day, Trammel even arranged for a special 10 a.m. "Sunday brunch" so the trainees could sleep in and relax as they woke up. After the trainees had slept in, then eaten brunch, Trammel commended them—those who had endured through the course.

"The SERE course is a test of commitment and intestinal fortitude. You now know yourself and your limits better, and I will repeat my words from our first day together: If you decide now that you are not suited to this work, please come to me personally, and we'll see you home. There's no shame in knowing oneself."

Not a trainee budged.

THEN IT WAS MONDAY again, the start of another week.

This week and four more, Laynie told herself as she plodded into the classroom.

Chin, an enigmatic smile creasing his face, stood before the class. "Welcome to Week 10—all fifteen of you."

"Wahoo," Taylor snarked and twirled a finger.

Laynie half smiled and gave him a thumbs up.

"Beginning today," Chin said, "your daily classroom and firearms training will come together in what we call scenario-based learning. For your introduction to scenario-based learning, you will spend an hour, every day this week, practicing your firearms skills within Little London."

The trainees roused and slid glances around, mouthing, "Little London?"

"You've seen Little London from the road during your morning runs; you've wondered what it is and what it is for. Here is the answer to both of those questions: We constructed Little London to resemble an urban city and function as one. Every element required to simulate a real operating environment is authentic, right down to the parking meters on the curbs, the garbage cans in the alleys, the shops and the apartments.

"We have, furthermore, populated the city with fully dressed mannequins and have designed urban shooting scenarios *in situ* by adding pop-up, cut-out targets that are either innocent bystanders or real bad guys."

Laynie's pulse quickened. Out of the corner of her eye, she saw Black smirking at her.

Well, that's because I'm grinning, too! Laynie covered her mouth with her hand and hid her smile behind it.

"Starting this afternoon, we'll be pulling you from your daily routine and rotating you through the shooting scenarios one at a time. An hour a day for fifteen trainees means some of you will shoot early and others late in the day. Also, for safety reasons, you will not use guns or live ammo. Instead, you'll use specially manufactured 'bean' shooters, the guns' color, LEO (law enforcement officer) blue, signifying that they are training weapons.

"Check the assignment board daily and report at the foot of the road leading to Little London five minutes before your assigned time slot. Wear full range gear."

The trainees, their spirits somewhat elevated, whispered and talked among themselves.

"Listen up, trainees! I've described the initial use of Little London. We'll run you through a week of urban firearms training, then move on. I think you'll find the second phase . . . a bit more interesting."

Excited to hear more, Laynie leaned forward.

"In Week 11, you will engage in individual and team scenarios where you must put your tradecraft into practice to complete your assignments. You will have ample opportunity to hone your skills through these realistic exercises. You will also have opportunity to identify your weaknesses and strengthen them.

"The scenarios will be simple and straightforward to begin with—but they will grow in size, scope, and complexity. The scenarios will, eventually, test every skill you've been taught. They will force you to solve problems and innovate in the moment, adapt to changing circumstances, and utilize your SERE training."

Utilize our SERE training? Laynie's excitement boiled away as she allowed herself to consider what it implied.

Chin, in his signature stance, hands on his slim hips, looked them over and seemed to confirm what Laynie had realized. "Let me be clear: The training scenarios will start off easy, but they will continuously evolve, requiring that you, too, continuously evolve. Set your minds now to roll with the punches because, beginning next week, when all training shifts from classroom to the field, *nothing will be off limits*."

LAYNIE'S FIRST ROTATION through the urban firearms training course was at 3:00 that afternoon. She stationed herself at the bottom of the road leading to Little London five minutes early and waited. A golf cart came for her.

At the top of the hill, she got out and was greeted by Benelli and de Guerre. They positioned her at the start of the course and familiarized her with a bright blue "bean" shooter.

"Just because your firearm shoots single plastic pellets, doesn't mean you ignore firearms safety, eye protection, or any piece of your training. Any projectile fired at high velocity will bruise skin or could put out an eye. Got it, Magda?"

"Got it."

"This is a diagram of Little London. You will traverse this street, turn left at the first corner, turn right at the next two, returning to the top of this street and back to us. As you sweep your way through the course, bad guys and civilians will pop out at you. Shoot the bad guys; don't shoot the innocent civvies."

"That's it?"

"That's it this time out."

When Laynie returned, having taken out eleven bad guys and almost killing a school kid who "jumped" out behind her, she was in love.

"Like it?" Benelli asked.

"Can't wait to do it again!"

He laughed. "Oh, you'll be doing it again, I promise you. *Lots* more."

THE TRAINEES WORKED through the same course and then more difficult variations of the course all that week. Repetition and practice calmed the trainees' adrenal responses; soon they were operating on their training and muscle memory without an accompanying rush of adrenaline. Laynie discovered that she was gaining a cool confidence in herself, her marksmanship, and her judgment.

During the eleventh and twelfth weeks of the program, the instructors pushed the students harder: they formed the trainees into squads of four and put the squads through exercise after exercise, all conducted within the artificial town. The instructors had developed the scenarios to challenge and strengthen the students' tradecraft, their problem-solving skills, and their tenacity. Each succeeding scenario grew in difficulty and danger.

The staff often ran overlapping exercises, meaning a trainee from one squad might encounter a trainee from another squad while conducting differing operations. In those instances, trainees had to pretend that the other squad's member was part of the backdrop. They learned to ignore the other squad—that is until the scenarios suddenly shifted, pitting the squads against each other, adding yet another level of complexity and hazard.

The trainees' days now extended well into the night so they might train under cover of darkness. The staff gave their students little time to eat and intentionally denied them adequate sleep; they pressed them, demanding more, making the students confront their weaknesses and defeat them.

After six days of nonstop scenario-based exercises, Trammel gave the trainees another Sunday as a day to rest and recuperate. He even ordered a second "you've earned it" late-morning brunch to go with the day of rest.

At the brunch buffet, Laynie heaped her plate high with bacon, sausages, hash browns, scrambled eggs, and large, chilled shrimp. She stacked three waffles on another plate and added two tall glasses of orange juice to her tray before she left the buffet line to sit down.

With fifteen trainees left, the dining hall was down to three tables of five. Laynie joined Black, Steph, Taylor, and Nora. They were the only table to have its original members.

"Lookin' mighty 'cut' there, Mags," Taylor purred in his lazy way. "Lean and mean."

Laynie was busy stuffing her face. Sure, she'd lost some weight and, in its place, built hard muscle, but she hadn't given it much thought. She was focused on finishing the course—right after she gorged.

"Oh? Guess I've lost a few pounds."

"We all have," Nora said quietly.

Something in Nora's tone snagged Laynie's attention. She slid her eyes to the British woman. Nora, fork unmoving in her hand, stared at her plate.

"Right you are, Nora. We've been running and gunning from dawn to dusk—and beyond."

Laynie looked around to gain the table's attention, then tipped her head toward Nora. "Of course, we've all dropped some fat. In its place, we've added muscle mass and gained strength. The harder they've pushed us, the harder we've had to lean on our training, right?" She looked directly at Black, who nodded once to show he understood.

"That's right," he said. "Whatever comes our way next, we have only two weeks of it left. Every one of us at this table has what it takes to finish."

Nora lifted her head. Tears stood out in her eyes. "Not sure, guys. Not sure I can do this anymore."

Steph and Taylor, on either side of Nora, gripped her shoulders.

"You *will* finish," Taylor murmured, "if you don't give up. Get those quitting words and ideas out of your head, Nor. Don't allow yourself to even consider giving up—not now, not after all you've accomplished."

"You were one of us, Nora, when we pledged," Steph added. "*Whatever the cost*—that's what we vowed: Whatever it costs, we're going to finish this course—and just look at us! We're the only intact table left."

Laynie could see that Nora appreciated the friendship and comradery extended to her, but a battle raged within, and no amount of support on the outside could fix what she was struggling against inside. Unless Nora herself dug deep and made the determination that she would gut it out and pay the price asked of her, she would either quit . . . or Marstead would scrub her.

Not me, Laynie told herself. *No matter what, not me.*

Nothing mattered more to her than finishing the course.

Chapter 10

Crash Week

THE FOLLOWING MORNING, the start of the course's second-to-last week, the trainees discovered why they'd been given a day to "rest up." To their amazement and dismay, Little London was no longer a faux town: Overnight, it had gone from mock-up to real.

Sometime during the previous night, while the trainees slept, additional Marstead personnel—so-called "adjunct instructors"—had quietly flooded onto the campus and taken up residence in Little London. Overnight, they had replaced the city's cutout figures and inanimate mannequins with a population of some fifty living, breathing, active humans.

Little London residents walked the sidewalks, operated vendor carts, drove vehicles (*even a short bus!*) through the streets, lay in dark corners as homeless drunks, and stepped in and out of shops and apartments. Doors slammed and people talked; music poured from the bar as patrons went in and out, cars revved their engines, drivers honked. The transformation was so complete and believable, it was unsettling. Unnerving.

The trainees' first foray into the transformed Little London jolted them.

"Welcome to Crash Week," Laynie whispered to herself as an unexpected car sped by, forcing her to jump out of the street and onto the curb, "where we trainees have ample provocation to crash and burn."

The regular instructors made no reference to Little London coming alive, as if not a thing had changed. As for the trainees, they knew better than to make mention of or ask about Little London's transformation; they were expected to adapt to changing circumstances and complete the mission. Period. The agents-in-training were required to succeed—no matter what. Those were their orders.

While the trainees struggled to adjust to these unpredictable and way-too-authentic mission parameters, Little London's citizenry did not. The population of the town acted their parts; they even interacted with the trainees—hawking their wares, engaging them in conversation, asking them questions, directions, or favors.

"Hotdog? Chili dog?"

"May I have a moment, young man? Could you tell me how to get to 521 Swisher Street?"

The citizenry of Little London had no regard for the scenarios. They asked for money or cigarettes or directions to the library at the most inopportune moments. They lurked around corners and lingered inside doorways, waiting to startle, to bump, to "accidentally" stumble into a trainee—and lift from a pocket the intel the trainee had just recovered.

During night exercises, Little London residents tried to mug or assault trainees. They posed as good cops and crooked cops, as drug dealers, pimps, and whores, even as lost children.

And any citizen, the trainees began to realize, could be the enemy in disguise.

WHEN THEY WERE allowed to eat late that night, Black admitted, "I about messed my pants when some guy came up behind me and asked for a light. Felt like I'd dropped into that movie, Night of the Living Dead, that nearby graves had opened up and the undead had found their way into Little London."

Nora grimaced. "Ugh. Don't tell me you watch that bilge."

"Okay, I won't tell you."

ON DAY TWO, TRAINEES were singled out and assigned missions with experienced operatives, complete strangers to them, but whose skills and loyalties the trainees were told to place their faith in. At first, the experienced operatives designed and directed the operations, giving the trainees a view into their expert methods.

Later, the trainees were given their own teams and were issued mission objectives. The scenarios called for the trainees to design the operation, assign their teammates to operational positions, and bear responsibility for the results: either a job well done or a failed exercise.

Now, as the trainees moved within the city, they ran actual SDRs (surveillance detection routes) to identify and lose real "tails." They avoided detection and fought through very real ambushes. If fired upon, they fired back.

The instructors had added “capture” to the exercises, too, forcing the trainees to rely upon their SERE training. When a student was captured, he found out, to his dismay, that Little London had its own interrogation facilities.

Their captors put a hood over the trainee’s head and dragged him down into a basement dank with moisture—or they drugged the student when she was apprehended, and the student awoke, hours later, on the cold, unforgiving concrete floor of a pitch-black cell, somewhere underground. Either way, the unlucky students who failed to evade apprehension endured hours of “persuasive” interrogations that tested their resolve.

Of course, “luck” had nothing to do with it. No matter what a student did, the deck was stacked against him or her. The trainee was betting against the house, *and the house always won*: No trainee was allowed to escape the mandatory testing of their resolve.

Adding on to the SERE course, the students’ captors followed the current scenario, questioning their prisoners regarding their identity, their agency, and their mission objectives. When students refused to cooperate, their captors stripped them and poured ice water on them. The trainees sat or laid on the wet cement for hours—or they were strung up by their hands, hanging from the ceiling until their arms and shoulders burned then went numb.

Most important, they had to accomplish their missions: If they “died” during a scenario, *they failed*, and too many scenario failures would get them scrubbed.

The trainees worked around the clock, with little time to sleep or eat, running op after op, role after role, until Laynie felt as though she were caught up in a dream. When her cognitive functions grew sluggish and faltered, the subconscious, proficient part of her mind—that combination of continual, repeated training and its complementary muscle memory, bordering on near instinct—locked in and took over.

It was then that Laynie began to trust herself; she learned to listen to her gut, plan on the fly, issue clear and succinct orders, hit the enemy hard and fast, demand more from herself than she had left in the tank, survive the loss of teammates, and push her remaining crew to ultimate success. She didn’t notice when her fellow trainees began to rely upon her leadership, to naturally turn to her for direction.

For Laynie, the rush of each fruitful exercise was addictive. Her personal need to succeed drove her forward.

So did her fear.

During "Crash Week," Laynie's predictions came true: Three more trainees washed out, folding under the ongoing pressure so completely that the instructors' consensus was to boot them from the program.

Nora was one of them.

Laynie grieved over Nora's departure, but the loss of her friend only fueled Laynie's absolute resolve to pass. Nothing terrified her more than the specter of failure, of Marstead scrubbing her from the selection process.

She went from telling herself, *I cannot quit; I must not fail*, to *I will not quit; I will not fail*. When she reached the point where she could hold out no longer, when her exhaustion teased her to surrender, it was that mantra that she repeated. *I will not give up. I won't.*

THEN THE WEEK ENDED, and it was Sunday, the trainees' half-day off. They'd just finished dinner. Ordinarily, they had the cool of a Sunday evening to play basketball, volleyball, or soccer or to sit around, tell jokes, and have a few laughs. Instead, following dinner, the instructors herded them into the briefing room where, six evenings of the week—but never on Sundays—they gathered for the daily AAR.

Something was up.

Trammel stood at the podium and addressed the trainees, only twelve in number.

"Listen up, people. Tomorrow begins the final week of your training. Those of you who are still here, who have gutted out the challenges we've presented to you and who have won through to victory? You should be proud. You have learned and grown tremendously. Your lives will never be the same because of all you have gained and proven to yourselves these past thirteen weeks.

"Training will continue through the coming week, but we will cease scenario-based exercises and focus only on perishable skills: physical fitness and firearms proficiency. In the morning, you'll see a marked adjustment to the schedule—blocks of time carved out for each of you to meet, one on one, with a panel of Marstead staff members.

"During these periods, we will evaluate your overall performance and where, in our estimation, you might fit best in our organization. These sessions will be a glimpse into your possible probationary assignment, your country of operation."

Laynie could scarcely breathe. Trammel had practically said the remaining trainees would be hired!

His words were not lost on Laynie's fellow trainees either. They moved with restless energy, the same excitement Laynie felt.

"Your panel will also discuss with you the areas in which your in-country training might focus—certainly additional tradecraft, but also language, the customs and culture of your country of operation, any area of perceived tactical, operational, or personal weakness."

He paused to consider the wording of his next statements. "During this week, Marstead will extend offers of employment to you. However, not all of you will receive offers to come aboard as probationary field operatives. A few of you will be offered support personnel positions."

Laynie was thunderstruck. Her heart hammered in her chest.

What if Marstead doesn't consider me worthy of a field position? What if they offer me a job as support instead?

She held her head still in rigid denial. *I don't want a support position. But what if they decline to make me a field offer?*

What will I do then?

Her fellow trainees were similarly disturbed by Trammel's statement.

"Settle down, trainees!" Trammel's voice cracked like a whip, cutting through the agitation and fidgety movement in the room.

"As I was saying . . . you will appear before a panel, and each panel will consist of three staff members who will question you extensively. Your panel will discuss with you any areas of perceived tactical or operational weakness. These weaknesses may be subjective, the observations of a single panel member *or* the concerns of *any member of our staff* conveyed to your panel. The panel participants may discuss their personal assessment of your character or a concern they have regarding your willingness to fully embrace the life of an operative.

"I wish to be clear with you: This process is not to be rushed or conducted in a *pro forma* manner. You will meet with your panel twice this week, and you will have ample opportunity to consider and address their concerns. However, at the end of the week, if even one panel participant or staff member has reservations regarding your fitness or suitability for field work? Their vote will be considered when determining whether the probationary position offered to you is in the field or in support . . . or if we will release you."

He gathered his notes. "Word of caution: You are not to discuss your panel experiences or outcomes with other trainees. That is all. See you in the morning."

Whether the position offered to you is in the field or support . . . or if we will release you?

The trainees stirred and started to get up, but Laynie put her elbows on the table and sank her face onto her hands.

Black tapped her elbow and put his mouth near her ear. "Hey. Hey, Mags. Listen to me. You don't have a thing to worry about. Honest. It's just one more test—don't let them rattle you, okay?"

Laynie lifted her face, took a deep breath, and nodded. "You're right. They're still trying to get in our heads."

"Yeah, well, they got in mine," Steph whispered.

Taylor moved around to the front of the table and huddled with them. "They got in all our heads, Steph, but only for a moment, right?"

"Right." Steph put on a bright, strained smile.

The fact was, they were all strained, all weary. They'd endured and pushed through so much.

"I think the best way to handle this newest curve ball is to get a good night's sleep," Black declared, "so I'm going to shower, then hit the rack."

"'Night, Black," Laynie murmured with the others.

CHAPTER 11

LP

IMMEDIATELY AFTER PT Monday morning, every trainee made a beeline to the dining hall to check the schedule. Of the trainees still in the program, three had two-hour panel sessions marked for the morning, three in the afternoon; the same was true for Tuesday. Laynie's first panel session was scheduled for Tuesday afternoon.

The trainees—except those scheduled for panel evaluations—spent the morning running obstacle courses, lifting weights, stretching, and in hand-to-hand matches. Laynie fought to keep her mind on what she was doing—and off the panel evals—but she wasn't alone in her efforts.

At noon, she and her friends entered the dining hall and watched for the three trainees who had met with their panels that morning. It was Laynie and her friends' unspoken hope to garner insights from observing the returning trainees. Only two of them showed up.

The class was down to eleven.

"It's Brett," Laynie hissed through her teeth. "He's the missing one."

Steph, Taylor, Black, and Laynie looked at each other.

"Released, you think?" Steph asked.

"That or he refused a support position," Taylor thought aloud. "Either way, he's gone."

The two trainees who did join them at lunch after their panel evals, smiled tight smiles and said nothing.

"'Cause we're not supposed to 'discuss our panel experience or outcomes with other trainees.'" Black repeated what Trammel had told them, what the others were already thinking.

Taylor, leaning back in his chair, one arm slung over the back in his casual manner, said, "I'm wondering about something."

Black glanced up. "Yeah?"

"Well, I notice that none of *us* are on the schedule until tomorrow and, face it, we are no slouches, as you Americans put it. I fully expect the four of us to pass and receive assignments. And so, I'm wondering if they are calling in the second-tier trainees first."

"Second-tier trainees? I like your thinking—if it's right." This from Steph.

"I agree with Tay. We've scored high on all our tasks and skills. I can't believe they wouldn't pass us," Black said. "But it's a crying shame we can't share our panel evals with each other. 'Anonymity' and all—said with sarcasm, of course."

Laynie chewed on the end of her thumb, mulling over their situation. "I, for one, won't disobey Trammel's 'word of caution.' But . . . but while he did say we were not to *discuss* our experiences or outcomes, what if . . . what if the four of us were to devise a signal, something only we would recognize, to let the others know we've passed our evals? No discussion; nothing more than a sign that we've passed and been offered a probationary field assignment."

She sighed. "You know, after this week, we won't see each other again, ever. I would really like to know if my mates—" she smiled at their three dear faces, "*my friends*—made it through."

"Gutsy move, Mags," Black said. Then he sniffed. "So, what's the signal?"

Taylor and Stephanie looked to Laynie and nodded their agreement.

"A simple word, I think. I mean, we're all beat, right? Due a vacation? And we'll be home for Thanksgiving and Christmas, more than a month. How about something along the lines of, 'I really need a vacation. I'd spend a month in Hawaii if I could swing it,' the key word being 'Hawaii.'"

With a casual glance around to ensure that no one was paying attention, Taylor murmured, "Any phrase with Hawaii in it?"

"Yup."

"Got it."

TUESDAY AFTERNOON, Laynie reported to her panel evaluation. It was to take place on the other side of the campus in the lodge, the very classroom where she'd signed her NDAs. A staff member drove her across to the lodge and accompanied her inside.

Laynie knocked on the door and a female voice called, "Enter."

Laynie walked in and closed the door behind her. A chair sat before a table. At the table were seated Ms. Stridsvagn, Gunny, and Mr. Henry, the rangemaster.

"Take a seat, Magda," Ms. Stridsvagn told her.

Laynie did so, slipping into her interrogation mode at the same time: Nothing she didn't want them to see would cross her face. Her expression serene, she faced the panel, her hands folded in her lap.

Gunny began first. "Magda, I first noticed your aptitude for problem-solving on the run during your exam weekend. Your innovative approach at getting you and your mates," he consulted the paper before him, "your colleagues, Chuck and Stephanie, up the last climbing wall as a team, demonstrated both thinking on the fly and leadership.

"As you've progressed during this training program, you have not disappointed. You have earned top marks in every tradecraft scenario, exhibiting growth in leadership and clear thinking under pressure.

"You are physically fit, and your SERE scores are also above average, particularly your cool head and disingenuous responses during interrogations."

Gunny went on, listing Laynie's accomplishments and praising her tradecraft. "It is my opinion that you will make a fine agent, perhaps even an exemplary one."

Mr. Henry spoke next. "Your firearms marks are satisfactory in every respect, and you have demonstrated familiarity and competence with the weapons we've provided for training.

"I also have here the reports from your hand-to-hand instructors. You've shown the same competence in close-quarters combat as you have in firearms, problem-solving, and leadership.

Ms. Stridsvagn went next. "As Gunny reported, you are in fine shape. Your physical exam tells us that you are in excellent health with no known defects, diseases, or conditions at this time. Your psychiatric exam also revealed nothing of concern: You appear to be a well-adapted individual with a strong sense of self-determination and strength of will.

"It is my opinion, too, that you would make a fine field operative."

Laynie allowed herself to breathe. To let down. "Thank you. And my assignment?"

Letting down was a mistake. Stridsvagn's next words would have sent her into a tailspin—three months ago.

But not now. Not anymore. Never again.

"Magda, two of our staff members have expressed a concern that we would like to discuss with you."

As Ms. Stridsvagn spoke, Laynie kept her facial movements relaxed. She breathed normally, did not lick her lips or permit her hands to twitch or move. Neither did she clench them. They remained gracefully posed, one across the other, atop her thighs.

Laynie nodded. “Of course.”

“Marstead is a secular organization. We don’t discourage the religious beliefs or leanings of our agents. That is, unless we sense that the morality of those leanings would pose an insurmountable objection to certain . . . tasks that could be assigned to an agent.”

Laynie knew. Right then, she understood exactly where Stridsvagn was going. Still, she did not react in any way.

“You are twenty-two, is that right?”

The panel knew her age; it was a ploy leading up to the “objection.”

“Yes; twenty-two last April.”

“It is unusual for a young woman of your age to be a virgin.”

Ms. Stridsvagn observed Laynie closely, watched for her reaction. Laynie, on the other hand, watched Gunny and Mr. Henry for theirs. Their expressions did not change, but both of them shifted their gaze away from her.

Not as good at this as I am, are you?

“Is it?” Laynie asked the woman.

Ms. Stridsvagn didn’t answer Laynie’s question. Instead, she cut to the heart of the objection.

“We are not animals here at Marstead, Magda, but we are also not ostriches with our heads buried in the sand. We live in the real world where our enemies are people of unimaginable evil, and we must defeat them with every tool, every advantage at our disposal.

“Your file tells us that you did well in the SERE course and our simulated interrogations; however, we did not threaten you with the sorts of demeaning acts of torture and humiliation an enemy could use on a woman—*would* use on a woman—acts that would be particularly damaging to a woman who is, shall we say, inexperienced.”

Ms. Stridsvagn inclined her head toward Laynie. “I speak of the unacceptable risk you might pose to our organization should you be captured. This risk poses a serious impediment to your advancement to probationary agent status. *But* it is also an impediment you can choose to remove, although . . . the time to do so is short.”

Ms. Stridsvagn’s gaze sharpened. “Do you understand what I’m saying?”

Laynie flicked a glance toward Gunny and Mr. Henry. They were watching her now, their gazes hooded by lowered lids. Their impassive inspection angered her. She wanted to sneer at them, curse them . . . but Ms. Stridsvagn's warning, ringing in her head, restrained and terrified her.

If I am not careful, if I act out, if I don't give them what they want . . . they will scrub me from the program.

Without moving a muscle, she weighed and considered her options.

"*Laynie, our bodies are sacred things, made special by God for to glorify him. We keep our bodies pure and holy a'cause* **he** *is pure and holy.*"

Oh, Mama! The world has changed so much since you were a girl.

She stood on the verge of refusing Ms. Stridsvagn's "suggestion." But what then? What would she do if they sent her home, having failed? A dark gulf opened up before Laynie . . . her future if Marstead rejected her.

No! No, I've come so far, worked so hard, overcome so much. I cannot falter now.

Slowly, Laynie lifted her chin. She met Ms. Stridsvagn's piercing scrutiny with the bland, disinterested mask she'd put on when she entered the room.

"I will take care of it, Ms. Stridsvagn."

TAYLOR SET HIS TRAY on the table at dinner and mumbled for their ears only, "Looking forward to the holidays. Sort of wish I could spend some of it in Hawaii—I hear the snorkeling is great."

He had their attention. "Any of the rest of you have, uh, plans?"

Stephanie, trying hard not to outright grin, said, "Hawaii sounds great! I'd love to go, too."

Black nodded. "Nothing like a nice Hawaiian punch, right?"

They turned their attention on Laynie. She picked up her fork and addressed her food, so she didn't have to meet their questioning eyes or face their reactions.

"I haven't made any plans yet."

LIGHTS WENT OFF in the trainee hotel at ten. Laynie waited until 10:30 before she slipped out her door and down the hall, to knock at another trainee's door. She heard movement, shifting on a bed, the hasty pulling on of clothes and soft shuffling of bare feet across the floor.

The door eased open a crack. "Maggie? What are you doing up?"

"Shhh." Laynie pushed on the door, and he allowed her inside; she closed it quietly behind her. She couldn't see much of him in the dark—meaning he couldn't see her, either. For that, she was glad.

This was going to be hard enough.

"Black . . . we're friends, right?"

"Absolutely."

"I . . . I need your help."

She stalled out.

He shifted. "Help. Okay. Sure. Will I be breaking any rules?"

"No, I don't think so."

"Then I'm your man."

I'm your man? Laynie felt sick, but she couldn't back away.

"Someone objected to my . . . vacation plans."

"What? Are they crazy? What kind of objection?"

"Turns out, I can't go to . . . Hawaii, unless I-I . . ."

"What's the problem? What can I do?"

"It's that I . . . I'm a virgin, Black. They said I'd pose a risk . . . I don't think they'll pass me unless I, unless I . . . you know."

He stilled. Said nothing. She heard him swallow.

"I told them . . . told them I'd take care of it."

Laynie shivered. There it was. Out in the open.

He still didn't say anything, but his hand came up and rasped across the stubble on his chin. A nervous tell.

He muttered a one-word expletive.

"Yeah." Laynie agreed.

More silence.

"I trust you, Black. As a friend. So . . . with no strings attached, no expectations. Just please . . . help me."

LAYNIE LEFT BLACK'S room before dawn. She hadn't slept much . . . after. All in all, she didn't feel anything one way or the other. Because she was numb.

He'd been gentle. Kind. Patient. Still . . .

Not how I'd ever imagined it . . . the first time.

She reached her room, showered, and dressed for the day, only to wait another two sleepless hours before it was time to gather at the flagpole for PT.

"Hey, Mags," Steph called.

"Hey, Steph."

Júlio blew his whistle. He and Hristo set the pace, and Laynie put her body into motion, running with her squad, her mind somewhere else.

Nowhere. Free fall.

It doesn't matter. It doesn't matter. It doesn't matter, she told herself. *I won't let it. All that matters is passing my panel exam.*

But for reasons she didn't fully grasp, it *did* matter.

She shoved her feelings aside, pushed them down. Squashed them into oblivion. Finished PT, showered, changed, made it to breakfast on time.

Their table was quiet while they ate. Laynie was certain they were pondering her cryptic, "I haven't made any plans yet" remark from dinner last night.

Except Black. Maybe he was remembering last night, revisiting it, but he kept glancing her way, a frown puckering his forehead.

She ate what she could, then cleared her tray and went outside. Alone.

My follow-up eval isn't until tomorrow, Thursday. I have to gut it out until then.

And she did. She threw herself into every activity set before her, trusting her training, the skills and instincts it had forged in her over the past months. She pushed herself hard, then harder, attacking her objectives with a fierce determination.

Anything, so long as she did not have to think.

ANOTHER STAFF MEMBER drove Laynie to the lodge on Thursday where she reported for her second panel evaluation. To her surprise, Ms. Stridsvagn was the only staffer present in the classroom.

"Take a seat, Magda."

Laynie sat.

"At your first panel eval, we discussed the objection raised by two staff members against your entry into probationary agent status. Do you wish to address the objection?"

Laynie cleared her throat. "Yes. I can report that I've taken care of the impediment."

Ms. Stridsvagn nodded. "I'm glad to hear it. You are one of our most talented trainees this year, Magda, worthy of Marstead's long-term investment, and I would have hated to lose you."

She smiled wanly and held out an envelope. "Congratulations. Marstead extends an offer of employment to you as a probationary field agent. Here is a copy of the offer including salary and benefits. Please take a moment to study it, but notice that it does not bear your name, for the sake of continued anonymity while you are here. You will read it and return it to me.

"In its place, Marstead HR will send two copies of the same offer bearing your actual name to your home address. You will sign your acceptance on one copy and return it to HR; the other is yours to show your family, if you wish. You are to destroy that copy before leaving to your country of operation."

Laynie exhaled. "Thank you." She took the proffered envelope, opened it, and read the details, which were generous.

"I'm ready to outline your assignment and begin the necessary preparations, if you are, Magda. Would you join me at the table, please?"

"Yes. Of course."

Laynie took the chair next to Ms. Stridsvagn. She wasn't really surprised when the woman announced, "Your country of operation will be Sweden. You'll spend the next few years living in our linguistics center outside Stockholm where we will immerse you in Swedish language and culture."

"I have a question," Laynie said.

"Yes?"

"I was just wondering, why does Marstead go to the trouble of recruiting an American to take on a Swedish identity? Don't you have qualified Swedes?" She nearly added, "like Taylor," but caught herself.

"Ah, that is a good question, indeed, which deserves a twofold answer. First, as you know, Marstead is a joint U.S./NATO venture but, frankly, the U.S. side of the partnership is as great as the entire NATO side combined. And the U.S. side insists on being adequately represented in the field. Call it an 'apportionment equation.'"

"So, I'm a token American?"

"One of many. The second response to your question is that Sweden is not a NATO signatory. However, the country is well-placed, both geographically and politically, to facilitate the needs of our mission. Marstead built its largest European office in Stockholm precisely because of the country's political neutrality—and because of its proximity to, shall we say, a certain association of non-NATO signatory entities, an association with whom we wish to do business."

The Soviet Union. A sharp thrill ran down Laynie's spine.

Ms. Stridsvagn laid out a one-page bio. The header on the bio read, "Linnéa Sophia Olander."

"This is your Swedish identity, enough detail to cover you from London into Stockholm. According to your bio, you were actually born in the U.S. to Swedish parents, giving you dual citizenship. Your father worked for a Swedish company with an office in Boston. When you were age nine, your father died from lung cancer—he was a heavy smoker. Your mother returned with you to your parents' little village in Uppsala Province. You completed your *Grundskola*—your comprehensive school—there."

She looked up. "That part of your background should suffice, should anyone catch a touch of American in you and question it before you have been fully enculturated."

"Yes, I see."

"You then completed your three years in upper secondary school. Your mother died in a drowning accident the summer before you began your university studies. Living off the proceeds from your father's life insurance that your mother had saved for you, you attended Stockholm University where you completed a bachelor's program in International Business and Politics.

"Other than your parents, you have only a handful of distant relatives, whom you do not know. You also surrendered your U.S. citizenship the same year your mother passed away.

"All these pieces of your identity will be backstopped with verifying documentation inserted into the proper places. While you are living in our linguistics center, our instructors will take you on many field trips to orient you to the locations in your background as well as to Swedish geography, history, and culture."

Laynie's heart fluttered with excited anticipation, but she murmured only a short, "Okay."

"I should remind you, Magda: You cannot take any paper from this room or speak to anyone of your country assignment or in-country identity. Therefore, you must memorize this short bio while we are here."

"I can do that."

"Good. Your employment will commence on January 3—although as Linnéa Olander, you will have *no public connection* with Marstead until you have completed your approximate five years of in-country training. Publicly, Linnéa Olander's employment with Marstead is years in the future. Until then, Linnéa is to make no mention of Marstead."

What? Five years?

Ms. Stridsvagn must have sensed her dismay. "It is necessary for you to understand the long-term investment Marstead is making in you, Magda—a deeper investment than most operatives. We have big plans for you, plans that require us not to 'bring you out' into the public eye too soon, plans that require you to do your master's program at a school where you will have opportunity to meet and befriend foreign students.

"Until you are actually working in the field, half of your Marstead salary will go toward the expenses of training you—your room and board at the linguistics center, living expenses during your master's degree, travel and ground transportation, and so on. Retaining even half of your salary is still quite generous for the skills and experience you will garner in exchange.

"After you return home to your American identity, Marstead will send you plane tickets from Seattle to London. However, when you disembark in the London airport, one of our agents will meet you and provide you with new papers, a ticket to Stockholm, and a change of attire. Our people will also pick up and dispose of your American suitcase and whatever you have packed in it. In place of your suitcase, they will check through a bag under your Swedish name from London to Stockholm.

"In this way, you will undergo a complete metamorphosis so that, when your flight lands in Stockholm, everything about you is Swedish—your passport, driving license, shoes, suitcase, clothing, jewelry, and hygiene items. Everything.

"Because you will never see your American suitcase and its contents again, do not pack anything you treasure—leave those items behind to 'visit' during your annual leave."

Ms. Stridsvagn stood. "Come. Stand here, please." The woman pulled out a tape measure and took Laynie's measurements, right down to her shoe size.

"That should do it—providing that you don't gain weight over the holidays."

She eyed Laynie. "So, don't overindulge."

"I won't."

"Stand against that wall, please."

"That wall" was the white one opposite a camera mounted on a tripod. Laynie posed for several headshots until Ms. Stridsvagn was satisfied.

"Very good. Spend a few minutes now with your bio and flight instructions, particularly how to identify your contact in London. When you have committed them to memory, we will be nearly done."

Laynie took the bio and a single paragraph outlining how the swap would take place when she flew into London's Heathrow Airport. She mouthed the details five times.

"Finished?"

"Yes."

"One last thing: If you encounter difficulties of any kind, call this number. It is the Marstead employee line, staffed day and night. State your name and this designation: Alpha seven three three five. It is your employee number and will ensure that your call is routed to someone who can help."

Laynie repeated the phone number and then, "Alpha seven three three five."

"Yes. Your employee ID."

"Got it."

Ms. Stridsvagn extended her hand; Laynie shook it. "We may not meet again, Magda, but I'm happy you have joined our company. You deserve to be here."

"Thank you, Ms. Stridsvagn."

Laynie left the lodge, and her driver took her back to the main campus. It was almost lunch time. She hung around the dining hall until the remainder of the trainees arrived.

Ten showed up to lunch. Ten out of thirty!

The number would have been nine if I hadn't . . .

She shook herself. *I paid the price for Marstead's acceptance. It's done. Let it go.*

"Maggie?" Black stood at her elbow, concern creasing the brows under his dark hair. Taylor and Steph lurked not far away.

One corner of Laynie's mouth lifted. "I hear snorkeling is great this time of year . . . in Hawaii."

CHAPTER 12

LAYNIE FLEW BACK to Seattle the Saturday before Thanksgiving. She was both drained and wired at the same time. Physically and emotionally, she needed to recuperate from the fourteen weeks of grueling training—not to mention that, at present, she felt somewhat feverish and her backside and both upper arms ached like the dickens.

Five inoculations will do that.

Her mind, however, strained ahead to her move to Stockholm.

As the plane descended into Sea-Tac airport, Laynie looked back on her training with mixed emotions. She, Black, Steph, and Taylor had grown close—how could they have done otherwise? They had fought together through hardships and difficulties, forging a bond of comradery, loyalty, trust, and affection, yet she would likely never see them—or Nora—again.

Black, Steph, and Taylor.

The bus had arrived that morning and shuttled them to BWI. On the Departures curb, Laynie, Steph, and Taylor hugged, shed a few tears, and whispered good wishes to each other.

It had been worse—awkward even—saying goodbye to Black. His amber eyes had stared into hers, probing, seeming to expect something from Laynie that she could not give him.

"Are you all right, Mags?"

"Yes. Why wouldn't I be?"

She sensed he wanted to say more, but there was no time for saying anything further—and what would be the point? They were about to embark on different paths, paths that would never cross.

"Maggie, I—"

"No. Don't say it . . . but thank you, Black. Thank you." She hadn't planned to, but she brushed his cheek with a kiss—just a soft and quick touch of her lips.

He'd opened his mouth, then closed it, and Laynie had walked away. She pulled her suitcase toward her airline's check-in counter, denying the urge to turn, to steal a last glance.

At the memory, the tears Laynie had managed to hold back that morning trickled down her cheeks.

Push it down, Laynie told herself. *Force it down. Make it let go.*

But "it" didn't "let go."

I wasn't supposed to love you, Black . . . That wasn't part of the deal.

THE PLANE'S WHEELS bumped on the runway, signaling the end of her flight. She wiped her face, gathered her things, and disembarked. Collected her suitcase. Flagged down a cab. Stared into space all the way to her parents' home.

If saying goodbye to Steph, Taylor, and Black had been hard, her homecoming proved as difficult or more so. When she walked through the Portlands' front door and announced, "I'm home!" Gene and Polly rushed to embrace her—only to pull back in astonishment and, perhaps, a little alarm.

"Laynie-girl!" Mama exclaimed, catching Laynie's face in her gentle hands and stroking her cheeks in awe. "You so tanned up! And thin! Didn't they feed you?"

Although Gene pursed his lips to keep from speaking, Laynie saw the surprise in his eyes.

"I'm fine, Mama, Dad," Laynie assured them. "Honest! And I ate like a horse."

"You jest as brown as a field hand, sugar, as brown as when you lifeguard all summer! Look like you spent all your time outside."

"Some," Laynie admitted, "but not all, I can assure you. Loads of time in the classroom—which they offset by keeping us active. Marstead's health and wellness policy doesn't allow their people to turn into couch potatoes."

She carried her suitcase up to her bedroom, unpacked, then showered. When she'd dried off, she weighed herself. Then she stared at herself in the mirror and saw what her parents had seen: The body staring back at her from the mirror was lean, its sharp lines and edges evident. She'd dropped ten pounds of "fat," but in its place, she'd acquired hard, taut muscle and a complexion that glowed with health and vitality.

Laynie reached into her dresser and pulled out her favorite jeans. When she slid into them, they bagged in the waist and backside. She grabbed for a second pair—same thing.

This isn't going to get better.

She pulled in the waistband and pinned it; over the jeans, she donned a shirt long enough to hide the big safety pin.

Need to alter a few items—but no sense buying anything new since whatever I pack to take to Sweden will be gone when I arrive.

Sweden. She blew out a breath, dreading the moment she would tell her parents.

I'll wait a few days to tell them about my move, let them adjust a little to me being home.

She could afford to wait for the "right time." Yes, she needed to tell them soon, but Polly was so beside herself with joy at having "both my babies home for the holidays," that Laynie couldn't bring herself to derail Polly's happiness. Not yet.

It grieved Laynie to think that it might be her last time "home for the holidays," given Marstead's leave policy of one month a year, taken in the summer. But whenever Laynie laid out the life of a Marstead field operative and rethought her decision, she always arrived at the same conclusion: She wanted it.

It was Sammie, when he came home that evening, who took one look at her and put his and his parents' wonderment into words. "Holy smokes! What in the world have you done to yourself, sis?"

Laynie and Polly were in the kitchen fixing dinner; Gene was within earshot.

"I'm just fitter than I was last summer," Laynie replied. "There was a gym and an obstacle course next door to the training facility we were at. The guys in class with me? They joined the gym and egged me on to work out with them. It's hard being a woman surrounded by so many macho and gung-ho guys; I didn't want to refuse and end up on the outside of their little clique. Besides, all that sitting around in the classroom would have made me soft. They joined the gym. So did I."

Sammie's eyes narrowed. "Joined a gym. Riiiight." He grabbed Laynie's elbow and steered her toward the back door.

"Hey!"

Laynie yanked on his grip, but Sammie was determined. He didn't know it, but his sister could have put him on the ground in one move—not something she wanted to demonstrate in the kitchen, in front of her parents.

She allowed him to pull her to the back of the yard to the big maple where, up in its wide branches, Gene had built them a treehouse when Sammie was six.

Sammie stopped when they were on the other side of the maple's thick trunk; he released her arm but got in her face.

"What *the devil* is going on, Laynie?" he demanded.

She put her hand on his chest and backed him away a few inches. "Whoa, Sam. Nothing is 'going on.'"

"The heck it isn't. You've been gone, what, three-four months? And you come back looking like-like-like . . ."

Laynie didn't know which shocked her more—Sammie employing as close to a curse word as she'd ever heard him use, or the fact that she'd left behind a little brother in August and had come back to a grown man in November.

She wasn't the only one to have changed over the summer and fall.

"Like what, Sam? Spit it out."

"Boot camp—that's it! You look like my buddy Mark did when he joined up and came back from basic . . . all cut and muscled, tanned and self-assured."

As though he'd spoken without thinking and, upon hearing his own words, had taken them in, Sammie blinked back sudden suspicion. "Laynie? Is that it? Have you joined the military? Is that it?"

"Good grief, no! I've joined a *company*, Sammie. They've offered me a job."

"I-I don't think I believe you."

"Well, it's true. I've received an offer, and I'm going to be moving . . . to Stockholm."

Distract, distract, she told herself, because no one in the world knew her half as well as her brother did.

"Stockholm? As in Sweden? You're moving *there?*"

"Yup. I leave right after New Year's."

"But . . ." Sammie stared at her, his gaze probing, seeking. "You're hiding something. You know you can tell me. I won't breathe a word of it to anyone."

Distract, distract.

Laynie leaned forward and rested her forehead on his. "Sammie. I know this is hard. We're growing up, little brother, and . . . and I'll be flying the nest soon," she whispered. "We have this time—Thanksgiving and Christmas—to enjoy as a family. Please. Let's be a family. Let's be together, while we can, okay?"

Sammie's arms came around her and hers around him. They hugged, and Laynie—to her amazement—rested her chin on Sam's shoulder.

"Wow! I think you've grown, Sam."

"Yeah. Put on another inch or two, but . . ."

"But?"

"But I still think you're not being totally honest with me, sis."

Laynie said nothing for a moment. She exhaled slowly before answering with a chunk of Marstead's boilerplate.

"Sam, my company is a worldwide leader in science and technology. Did you hear the words, 'worldwide leader'? Marstead doesn't just work on the cutting edge of some of the greatest advances the world has ever seen, it *is* that edge—and that makes them a big target for industrial espionage.

"The theft or sabotage of intellectual property by other companies, even other nations, is the chief threat they face. So, I had to sign a bunch of NDAs when I accepted their employment offer."

"NDAs? What are those?"

"Nondisclosure agreements. Binding contracts."

"*. . . You can expect us—and we promise—to rain hellfire down upon you and yours.*"

"The truth is, I'm not going to be able to tell you much about my work with them, not now, not in the future. I think you're always going to suspect that I'm holding out on you—for the simple reason that I am. You'll have to get used to it, I guess."

"Okaaaay . . ."

"And as far as me moving to Sweden? I mean, you're already in your sophomore year at UW and getting awesome grades; two more years, and you'll be out, looking for a job, too. Don't you want a bit of excitement in your life before you get married, settle down, start a family? Well, this is my chance."

"I suppose."

"You know I'm right. And it's normal. The whole 'circle of life' and all that? It's my time, Sammie. My time to fly away and have an adult life."

"I don't like it."

Laynie laughed softly. "No, I guess not. And neither will Mama and Dad. All the more reason for you and me not to ruin Thanksgiving and Christmas for them."

"When will you tell Mama and Dad?"

She stood back. "Next week."

"Talk about ruining Christmas for them . . ."

Laynie shook off his distressing words. "Nope. It'll be wonderful. Come on now, little bro. Dinner's probably ready, and I don't want to worry Mama and Dad."

"Fine. Only I'm not the little one anymore, am I?"

Laynie punched him in the arm.

"Hey!"

"You will *always* be my little brother—got it?"

Arm in arm, they headed back to the house.

LAYNIE'S OFFER LETTER and her tickets arrived in the mail the Monday after Thanksgiving. That was when Laynie gathered her parents and Sammie in the living room for a family meeting.

It had to be done.

"I wanted to tell you that Marstead confirmed in writing the job they offered me, the position I was hoping for."

"Where?" her mother asked.

"It's . . . it's in Europe, Mama. Stockholm, Sweden, to be precise."

Into the silence stretching between them, Laynie added, "It's a marvelous opportunity. I will get to travel. See the world."

Polly stared at her hands to hide the tears welling in them, but they dropped onto her lap anyway. Gene was calm. Stoic. Sammie clamped his mouth shut.

"When?" Gene finally asked.

"I leave January 3 . . . and there are a few other things I should explain to you."

Polly and Gene blinked in shock. Sammie, assuming his, "I don't believe you" stance, folded his arms and dared her with his eyes to utter anything other than the truth.

But nothing Laynie would say next was a lie. She'd been schooled on precisely how to answer her family's questions and concerns, and she had Marstead's written offer to back her up.

"First, I still have a lot to learn about this job, so I will be working and training concurrently for the next year. Second, if I do well and receive good evaluations, Marstead will pay for my master's program."

Gene and Polly perked up.

"Graduate school?" Gene asked. "You'd be the first in the family to earn a master's degree."

"Yes, and not just any grad program, either. Marstead will pay for my MS at The Stockholm School of Economics—that's the *Handelshögskolan i Stockholm* in Swedish. It's a really prestigious school, Dad. Like I said, if I do well for Marstead and stay with them, they will invest in me, in my career. It truly is a once-in-a-lifetime opportunity for me."

Gene and Polly slowly nodded their agreement.

She swallowed, working her way up to the rest of her news. "The thing about Marstead I should explain is that, although they have offices in just about every country across the globe, their biggest concentration of employees is in Europe. And having a predominantly European workforce, Marstead has developed a distinctly European company culture."

"What's that mean?" Sammie asked, irritation furring his words.

"Hold your horses; I am getting to it."

"Not fast enough."

"Stephen Theodor Portland," Gene admonished him.

Gene and Polly only used Sammie's real, full name when they meant business—just as they had used 'Helena Grace Portland' whenever Laynie got in trouble growing up.

"Sorry, Dad. Sorry, Laynie." His folded arms said otherwise.

"It's okay. I know this is a lot to absorb. What I am getting at is this: Marstead employees, in keeping with European customs, get a full month of holiday each year—which is wonderful, except it is always taken in summer, usually August."

"A month! Right generous of them," Mama said.

Then she "got it." When her breath hitched, Gene took her hand.

"But only in summer, you say? You cain't . . . you can't come home any other time? Not for Thanksgiving? Or Christmas? Ever?"

"A month, only in summer, and they will grant me a full leave this coming August but . . . but no, I won't be able to come home . . . any other time."

Gene drew Polly closer. "It will be all right, Polly; it will be all right. Part of growing up. It's time for Laynie to spread her wings."

CHRISTMAS AND THE DAYS leading up to it were more subdued than any other Advent season Laynie had experienced. To ease the coming separation, Laynie did everything her parents asked of her as they prepared for what, to them, was a holy day, not merely a holiday. She helped Polly clean, shop, bake, and cook. She prepared gift baskets for those in the church who were struggling financially; she served meals alongside Gene, Polly, and Sammie in a Seattle homeless shelter—she even caroled with their church choir at three nursing homes and attended Christmas Eve service without complaint.

Laynie did her utmost to ease the pain her departure would cause . . . while hiding her own rising anticipation. When she had a free moment, she slipped away to visit the nearest library, where she pored over atlases of Scandinavia and Swedish travel guides, absorbing a wealth of interesting facts.

Her forays to the library helped keep the preparations for Christmas mostly tolerable, except for one happenstance at church—an encounter with an older woman whom Laynie didn't at first remember.

"Laynie Grace Portland! My, I am glad to see you, little miss."

Laynie struggled to put a name to the face. "I'm sorry, ma'am?"

The frail, white-haired woman chuckled. "I've aged a mite since I taught Sunday school, I wager. You used to call me Miss Laurel when you were in my class."

The face and name, like two interlocking pieces, snapped together. "Miss Laurel! I . . . I'm sorry I didn't recognize you right off."

"It's no matter, dear. Been, what, twelve or more years since you were in my Sunday school class?"

"Yes; I think I was nine, so about thirteen years."

Miss Laurel sighed. "Lost a husband since then. Took a minute to get my feet back under me—a minute that lasted 'bout five years. In the meantime, I think I got old."

She laughed at her own joke, but Laynie didn't. Miss Laurel had aged. She had been a wise and spirited teacher, one of the best Laynie remembered, but she'd changed. If Miss Laurel hadn't spoken to Laynie, Laynie would not have known her.

"It's good to see you, too. I'm so sorry about your husband."

"Thank you. Thank you, child. But, I'm particularly glad to have seen you today."

"Oh? Why is that?"

Miss Laurel crooked her finger, beckoning Laynie near. When Laynie obliged, Miss Laurel whispered, "Because I was praying earlier this week, and had me a word from the Lord for you, Laynie Portland."

Laynie's mouth dried up; she ran her tongue around her gums and teeth, trying to conjure up some moisture. She frowned, too. It was exactly *that sort* of "magical" Christianity she disdained—people who declared that they "knew" God personally, "knew" him well enough to "hear" from him.

What she didn't perceive was the irony—how contrary, how contradictory, her beliefs were that she would, on the one hand, experience a physical reaction over "a word from the Lord" when, on the other hand, she considered the entire proposition nonsensical and phony.

Amid her denial, all her parched mouth could croak was, "Oh?"

"Yes, ma'am. I was praying—praying about something else entirely, you see. You, my dear, hadn't crossed my mind in months, maybe years, to tell the truth. Don't know what you've been busy with or about.

"But, just like that?" she snapped her fingers, "you dropped into my heart. And I felt the Lord prompting me to say something to you, but I thought, why, how could I tell you anything? Haven't seen you in quite a while, as you know."

She cocked an eye at Laynie, that silent chastisement for skipping church months on end.

"I've been out of town on business, Miss Laurel."

"And I figured I wouldn't see you this evening to deliver that word—but here you are."

Miss Laurel might have been old, but she was no fool; she saw beyond the good manners Polly and Gene had instilled in their daughter. Saw the flicker of contempt behind Laynie's smiling good nature.

"'Tis a simple word, Laynie, from Deuteronomy 11:16, needing no explanation." She patted Laynie's hand. "I am but the messenger and won't bore you none with repeating it. You look it up when you have time, all right?"

"All right. Thank you, Miss Laurel."

"You're welcome, Laynie. And a very Merry Christmas to you."

CHRISTMAS WAS OVER, all the preparations, activities, singing, churchgoing, and the wrapping and giving of gifts. The calm interlude between Christmas and New Year's descended. With Laynie's departure looming, Gene asked for a week of vacation time. Then Laynie, Sammie, and their parents enjoyed lengthy, quiet days of getting up or going to bed when they wanted to, of playing board games, assembling jigsaw puzzles, talking, laughing, and eating the bounty of their Christmas baking.

It was fun and memorable . . . and those memories would have to last Laynie a long time.

Early on New Year's Eve, hours before the fireworks began, Laynie began to sort out her room and pack her bag. She was taking only one suitcase, having been told that whatever she packed would disappear anyway.

"*Before you step foot on Swedish soil, Magda, you will undergo a complete metamorphosis so that, when your flight lands in Stockholm, everything about you is already Swedish—your passport, visas, driving license, shoes, clothing, jewelry, and hygiene items. Everything.*

"*Take only one suitcase with you on the plane, and pack whatever you wish, but be aware that on your way to Stockholm, as you pass through London, our people will dispose of your suitcase and whatever is in it. So do not pack anything you treasure—leave those items behind to 'visit' during your annual leave.*"

"Well, what do I want to take that I don't care if they confiscate?"

Laynie sifted through the detritus of her childhood and adolescence, setting aside what she would leave in her room, adding very little to her suitcase. In the end, she packed clothes that no longer fit her, hoping that, after Marstead removed the clothes from her bag, they would find their way to someone in need, someone who would appreciate them.

While rummaging through the nightstand drawer next to her bed, she uncovered her childhood Bible. She stared at it, the conversation with Miss Laurel as fresh as when it had occurred.

"'*Tis a simple word, Laynie, from Deuteronomy 11:16, needing no explanation. I am but the messenger and won't bore you none with repeating it. You look it up when you have time, all right?*"

Laynie slowly turned the pages until she found the "simple" word from the Lord in Deuteronomy that Miss Laurel had delivered to her. She read the short passage, and her breath caught in her throat, threatening to strangle her.

Miss Laurel was right. It needed no explanation.

Take heed to yourselves,
that your heart be not deceived,
and ye turn aside, and serve other gods,
and worship them.

Laynie slapped the Bible closed, likewise clamping down on the guilt caroming around like a loose bowling ball in her heart. She shoved the book and its convicting words into her nightstand drawer and slammed the drawer shut.

CHAPTER 13

JANUARY 3, 1978

IT WAS EARLY and still dark when Sammie loaded Laynie's bag into his car. Laynie hugged her parents and said goodbye to them. They had, somehow, made peace with her leaving.

Still, as her mother held her close, she whispered in Laynie's ear, "Laynie-girl, Dad and I will be praying for you ever' night and ever' day. We be holding you up to the Lord, asking him to keep you safe and keep you in his will."

As she whispered back, "Thank you, Mama," a sardonic heckler shouted in her head: *Won't it be kinda hard for God to* ***keep*** *you in his will, if you aren't there in the first place?*

Shut up, Laynie answered.

Gene Portland hugged Laynie next. "We love you, Laynie. Don't forget that."

"I won't forget. I love you, too, Dad."

Sammie drove Laynie to Sea-Tac to catch her 7 a.m. flight. He was mostly quiet during the drive, which suited Laynie. She was preoccupied with her own thoughts. It was when they arrived at the Departures curb that he said his piece.

"Laynie?"

She sighed. "What, Sam?"

"I don't believe you're just 'taking a job' in Sweden. I already told you that—and I'm sticking to what I said. But, having thought it over, I figure you can't tell me what it is you're really doing. So, just know . . . just know that whatever it is you're mixed up in, Mama and Dad aren't the only ones who'll be praying for you."

Laynie looked down into her lap, blinking back the sting of moisture. "Thanks, Sam."

"And you'll be back this summer, right?"

"Yes. August."

"Okay, well now that you'll be making the big bucks, can we plan to rent a little boat for a week while you're here? Get out on the Sound?"

Laynie sniffled. "I'd like that."

"Good," Sammie said. "I'll . . . guess I'll get your suitcase out of the trunk now."

Standing at the curb, they hugged.

Then Laynie took her bag and walked away.

MARSTEAD HAD BOOKED Laynie from Seattle to London with London as her final destination. Linnéa Olander was booked from London to Stockholm, and Marstead had built a two-hour window between the two flights, more than enough time to accomplish their purposes. Per her instructions, Laynie, her handbag slung crosswise over her chest, left her gate looking for her contact, an individual loitering nearby who would be holding a beige valise with a distinctive oxblood-leather monogram stitched to its side.

There. By the trash bin.

Laynie sauntered by the bin, eyes front and ahead. She dropped some wadded paper in the trash. At the same time, the woman with the bag turned toward Laynie, sliding by her. The pass was perfectly timed; when Laynie cleared the bin, she carried the bag by its handle. She then sought the women's restroom nearest her arrival gate and went in.

The restroom was busy, and all of the stalls were in use, so Laynie got in line. When a stall opened up, she went in, sat, and opened the valise. Inside, she found a complete change of clothes and a different handbag. Within the handbag she found a passport, airline ticket to Stockholm, a wallet containing a modest number of kronor, a letter of instructions, and several personal items.

"*Take everything off and dress entirely in the clothing and accessories provided. Exchange purses.* ***Take nothing from your old purse; take no old article of clothing or jewelry with you****. Put your old clothing and your purse inside the valise.*"

Laynie breathed deeply. *Nothing.* She would have nothing of her own when she left the restroom.

She stripped down and put on the clothing Marstead had provided. It all fit her, right down to the underwear and shoes.

Well, duh. They took all my measurements after fourteen weeks of training—because I'd lost weight.

She remembered Ms. Stridsvagn's mandate: "Don't overindulge."

Laynie dropped the letter into the toilet and watched it dissolve. When she had folded her discarded clothing and shoes into the valise, she added her old handbag and zipped the valise closed. She left the stall and went to the sinks to wash her hands. While there, she brushed her hair, then drew from her pocket the scarf Marstead had provided. She folded the scarf into a wide band that she tied over her hair and studied its effect in the mirror.

Laynie Portland had arrived in London and would go no further. In an hour or so, Linnéa Olander would depart Heathrow for Stockholm, Sweden.

As Laynie left the restroom and started down the concourse, the valise in her left hand, the same woman who had handed off the valise to her, swept by and carried the bag away.

The woman left in her wake a blonde Swede wearing the stylish scarf, repeating to herself,

Linnéa Olander. My name is Linnéa Olander.

THREE AND A HALF HOURS later, Linnéa deplaned in Stockholm's Arlanda Airport and headed for baggage claim. She'd been traveling for close to seventeen hours, having left the Pacific coast of the U.S. in the early morning yet arriving in Stockholm just after 4 p.m. because of the time change. She was tired.

Also, while it had been wet, dreary, and downright chilly in Seattle, from what Linnéa saw through the airport windows, Stockholm was in the grip of full-on winter, and she wore only a light sweater.

She handed her claim ticket to a baggage handler who returned with a suitcase much like her own, but one she'd never seen before. The case had an ID tag reading "Linnéa Olander."

Guess that's mine.

Linnéa led the baggage handler out of the airport to the Arrivals curb. There, Linnéa spotted a man with a placard reading, "Olander" and made her way to him.

While Linnéa tipped the baggage handler, the placard-holding man took her suitcase and put it in the trunk of a small car. He held the rear door for her. She slid in and found a nice parka waiting for her on the seat.

"*Tack.*" Thank you.

He nodded, then navigated out of the airport in silence and turned the vehicle onto an artery running south/southwest until it merged onto the E4, southbound. Linnéa, for her part, sat still with her head angled toward the window while her hungry eyes roved over the passing scenery. She knew the airport was about thirty-seven kilometers north of Stockholm's city center, about midway between Stockholm and Sweden's fourth-largest city, Uppsala.

The map of Sweden, from a distance and to the casual observer, appeared to have a solid outline. Close up, particularly the easternmost point of the country where it jutted into the Baltic Sea, the border of Sweden encompassed a maze of islands and interconnecting waterways—an archipelago. Linnéa knew that Stockholm itself was built on fourteen of those islands joined by fifty bridges. As her driver entered the city, Linnéa saw water everywhere she looked.

I'm used to water. Lots of it surrounding Seattle.

Eventually the driver drove into a parking garage and pulled into an unoccupied spot. He got out, and Linnéa saw him speaking to a woman.

The woman approached and opened Linnéa's door.

"*God middag,* Miss Olander. *Välkommen till Stockholm.* Come with me, please."

Linnéa slid from the rear seat and followed the woman. Her driver fetched her suitcase and trailed after, putting her case in a second vehicle.

"Please sit with me in the front seat where we can talk more easily," the woman said to Linnéa in Swedish. A moment later, they left the parking garage.

"My name is Annika Norling; I am the head of Marstead's linguistics center. You may call me Anna."

"Thank you, Anna," Linnéa answered.

"I think you'll find the 'house' comfortable, but we do have a few rules you should be aware of before we arrive. You are familiar with the first: Anonymity with regards to your previous identity and background. You are now Linnéa Olander. You have committed your brief bio to memory, *ja?*"

"*Ja.*"

"We will reinforce and build out your background as we go along. The second rule is this: no English from this point forward."

Annika slanted her eyes toward Linnéa. "We have been instructed to teach you Russian as well as Swedish."

Linnéa nodded. Annika's announcement did not surprise her.

"Since you will be studying Russian as well as Swedish, you may use either language in the house. However, we are to train you to look, think, and speak as a Swedish citizen. This will be your primary objective. Your assigned linguist will issue you a Swedish-English dictionary. If you cannot pose a question in Swedish, you must study out how to convey your meaning. The rule is meant to discourage anything but Swedish.

"The third rule is that, until we deem you able to pass as a Swede, you will avoid making acquaintances outside the house. For the time being, we will control your access to non-Marstead personnel. *Förstår du?*" Do you understand?

"*Ja, jag förstår perfekt.*" I understand perfectly.

"Your inflection is quite good."

"Thank you. My father—" Linnéa stopped. "Sorry."

"Make your mistakes now. They will not be tolerated once we reach the house."

She saw, when they arrived, that the 'house' had obviously once been a narrow three-story apartment complex containing six little apartments, two to a floor. Those overseeing the conversion to Marstead's linguistics center had combined the bottom two apartments to create single, larger living and dining areas and kitchen. The two bedrooms had been converted to classrooms.

They had taken the remaining four apartments—two on the second and two on the third floor—and expanded them to six apartments, three per floor, by excluding the kitchens and dining nooks from the original apartments and combining them to make one new apartment.

Linnéa's apartment was on the third floor. She had a bedroom, a tiny bath, and a small sitting area to herself but would take her classes and meals on the first floor.

From her front window, she looked out onto the street below and the rooftops of other narrow homes or apartments nearby; from her bedroom window, she stared across the alley three floors down and into a neighboring house so close, she felt she could reach across and join hands with its occupants. She drew the thick curtains, not relishing the idea of anyone looking in while she dressed or undressed.

"Your days," Annika explained as Linnéa unpacked, "will be full, from daybreak to nightfall. In the linguistics center, we do most everything together as a group, utilizing every task or outing as a learning experience. You will have classes with the other two residents three mornings a week—languages, history, art, music, literature, government and politics—and a variety of field trips in the afternoons and evenings to museums, concerts, galleries, and folk festivals."

"We share the household tasks—cooking and cleaning—and also the shopping. When it is your turn to cook, we will visit the markets where you will learn how to shop, haggle, and count Swedish money.

"To ensure that your tradecraft does not grow stale but continues to improve, probationary agents will report three times a week to another Marstead facility. The instructors there will continue your training, taking you out in the city to run exercises. In this way, you will hone your field practices and learn the city—its layout, important landmarks, how to navigate through it, and varying modes of transport.

"However, publicly, you will pretend to know little of Marstead International and have no known association with Marstead until their plans for you are ripe, until you are fully prepared for the role they have chosen for you—which may or may not be as a direct Marstead employee."

Linnéa listened, but she was sleep-deprived, jet-lagged, her thoughts drifting due to her long flight and the nine hour time difference between Stockholm and Seattle. She stifled a yawn.

Can't wait until they let me go to bed.

Annika must have seen her fatigue. "Come; let me introduce you to your housemates and the staff. Dinner is at 6:30 each evening, in about ten minutes. You may retire after you've eaten."

An hour later, as soon as she put her head on her pillow, Linnéa felt herself falling down a dark, welcoming hole. She slept so hard that her neck was stiff when a bell echoed up the stairwell the following morning, rousing her. Soon after the bell, Annika knocked on her door.

"Ah, Linnéa. I see you are up. Feeling rested?"

"Yes. I slept well."

"Good, good. Breakfast is in fifteen minutes. You will join us and begin your studies today."

AT BREAKFAST, LINNÉA met three instructors and two residents, Milo and Erika. By their accents, she pegged Erika as Danish and Milo as German. She nodded as they introduced themselves.

"Linnéa Olander," she replied. "*Trevligt att träffas.*" Pleased to meet you.

With that simple greeting, Linnéa moved into a seven-month stint in the linguistic center. She embraced the training but particularly looked forward to Tuesdays, Thursdays, and Saturdays when Annika drove the three students, Milo, Erika, and Linnéa, to a parking garage where they shifted over to another vehicle (always a different one) and were taken to the outskirts of Stockholm where Marstead owned a combination gymnasium and firing range.

Laynie was in her element there, as her instructors soon discovered. She was fit and agile, and she adapted quickly to whatever problem or exercise the instructors threw at her. As the exercises increased in complexity, the instructors moved their students into the city to run surveillance on randomly selected individuals, both pedestrians and drivers.

Laynie learned to conceal and carry a block of unstained wood carved into the simplistic replica of a small semiauto pistol. It was an appropriate size and weight to practice carrying a gun in a shoulder harness under a jacket, a holster at the small of her back, a holster strapped to the inside of her thigh under a skirt, or one strapped to her ankle when she wore slacks.

"Sweden's gun laws are not as restrictive as some European nations," their instructors told them, "but it is illegal for a civilian to carry a firearm for other than a specific, legal purpose, and the gun must be licensed. Transportation of a firearm requires that the gun be unloaded and hidden during transport.

"We do not want our agents, probationary or otherwise, carrying a firearm unless necessary—however, we do want you to know *how* to carry and keep your weapon concealed. A whole lot of covert operations consist of standing or sitting around, waiting, watching, listening, then waiting some more. But that one instance when your life is on the line? You will be grateful to have this skill, I promise you."

IN AUGUST, LINNÉA "transitioned" back to the States and her identity as Laynie Portland for her first annual leave. During her layover in the London airport, she was met by an agent who passed Linnéa her Laynie identification papers and took away her Linnéa papers. In this way, she entered the United States as Laynie Portland, leaving Linnéa behind.

Once home, to avoid in-depth conversations about her work with Marstead, Laynie spoke at length on Swedish culture, the sights she'd seen and history she learned while walking the streets of Stockholm. Gene loved it and enjoyed speaking Swedish with her, marveling at how her facility with the language had far outstripped his.

"You sound just like a native speaker, Laynie," he praised her.

Good, she thought.

Sam took a week off from his summer job and, as they had discussed, he and Laynie rented a little two-man sailboat and took it out on the water every day of that week.

"I'm saving my money," she told him. "After you graduate, let's buy that boat we've dreamed about, okay?"

She was sorry when that wonderful week of sailing ended and Sam returned to his summer job. After that, she only saw him in the mornings or evenings. With Sam unavailable, the remainder of her month-long leave stretched before her, another three weeks of it. Laynie intentionally avoided old friends and acquaintances, and that left her with nothing more to do than spend each day puttering around the house and yard with Polly while Gene was at work.

"Let's take some drives," Laynie suggested, "see some sights together."

Polly took to the idea, and they made day forays to scenic or interesting locations while Gene worked—a day over Chuckanut Drive, another through the Whidbey Scenic Isle Way, a morning at Pike Place Market, and getting massages together—something Polly resisted, then gave in to when Laynie insisted.

"Oooh," Polly moaned in delight. "Never had a massage before. So good, 'tis almost sinful, Laynie-girl."

Laynie laughed. "Told you you'd love it, Mama. And—oh! Oh, right there, no, *there*. A little more of that, please!"

Polly giggled like a girl and sighed with happy contentment. A minute later she whispered, "Thank you for taking me out of the house and spending time with me, Laynie. I sure am having the time of my life with you, sugar."

"Me, too, Mama. Me, too."

And Laynie, in that moment, experienced a revelation of sorts, that these day trips, just mother and daughter—trips Laynie had initially devised to alleviate her boredom—were actually precious moments she would treasure when she returned to Sweden. Laynie also realized that nothing had ever prevented her from doing this when she lived at home, that she and her mother could have shared a wealth of these priceless moments . . . *if I hadn't been so all-fired anxious to leave, to get away.*

"I'll miss you and Dad when I go back, Mama."

"We'll miss you, too, sweet girl. I take my comfort in knowin' that wherever you go, Jesus goes with you, Laynie. He will never, ever leave you, sugar. He done made that a promise."

Polly's words irritated Laynie and stole the pleasure of their outing, but she didn't reply. She couldn't bear to wound her mama.

Oh, Mama! How can you believe such nonsense? You don't know the real me. If you knew the truth, it would break your heart.

Jesus isn't "with" me! How could he be?

I am not worth his time.

LAYNIE WAS GRATEFUL for her time home, but the month passed, and Sweden beckoned to her. She was anxious to return . . . because, her instructors had told her before she left, they had received permission to begin to use her for simple mission tasks—pickups, deliveries, surveillance relief, and the like.

"You're doing well, honing your skills," they told her. "You are going to make a fine operative in time."

In time. It was what kept Laynie determined, kept her focused. Achieving the goals Marstead set out for her and thereby earning their trust and respect was her only path forward.

Her efforts also kept her from feeling the deep, pervasive loneliness that, if she allowed it to, crept into her thoughts and her emotions.

The hard work kept her from hearing Mama's voice in her head, "*Wherever you go, Jesus goes with you, Laynie. He will never, ever leave you, sugar. He done made that a promise.*"

"I didn't ask for you to 'go with me,' to stalk my every move," Laynie hissed when the voice persisted. "I didn't ask for you in my life.

"*Just leave me alone!*"

Laynie Portland
SPY RISING

PART 2: LINNÉA

LP

CHAPTER 14

LP

STOCKHOLM, SWEDEN, AUGUST 1981

LINNÉA LOCKED THE DOOR of her apartment behind her and set down her suitcase. *Home again.*

She scanned her bare apartment and sighed. Marstead had transitioned her back to the U.S. for her annual leave two weeks early this year, as they had last year, to accommodate the classes in Linnéa's master's program that began the third week of August.

It had been a nice visit home. Mama and Dad were in good health, although Mama seemed to tire easily.

"I'm all right, Laynie-girl. Just a mite weary."

Laynie, not entirely convinced, had sought out Gene. "Dad, is Mama okay? She seems a little off."

"I know, I know. She's been stumbling some, too, but she never complains. I haven't been able to get her to see the doctor about it until recently. We have an appointment for her in October."

"You'll let me know what he says?"

"Yes, of course."

Laynie had been able to answer their questions about school and pass off their queries about Marstead with simple, pat replies. She was yet to be employed by Marstead as Linnéa, but the cover story her parents believed had Laynie working out of Marstead's Stockholm office going on four years now.

Then there was Sam. While some things at home seemed to never change, others did. With his degree behind him, Sam had taken a job he enjoyed and had rented his own place to live. And in February, he had found the little two-man sailboat they'd dreamed of buying together.

"Let's get it, Laynie," he'd written to her. "I can have it seaworthy when you come next summer."

So, Laynie had sent him half of the boat's price plus extra to refit sails and tackle. Sam had spent his spring weekends stripping the old paint, sanding the hull smooth, repainting it, letting the paint cure, then hand-lettering the boat's name on its stern in flowing red script: *The Wave Skipper*.

Laynie had been delighted when first she set eyes on the boat. "Oh, Sam! It's perfect."

"Yeah, well, she's little, maybe not much to boast about in the looks department, but the 'Wave Skipper' part? Totally right on. Can't wait for us to take her out together."

He'd scheduled a week of vacation during her visit, and they'd sailed out of Lake Union and west across the length of Salmon Bay, then motored through the Ballard Locks out onto Puget Sound. They'd flown across the Sound's chop and danced atop the waves, proving the worth of their little sailboat's name.

A good visit, indeed. A needed distraction.

With a sigh, Laynie hauled her suitcase into her bedroom to unpack. She was relieved that classes would start up again soon, that her push forward would continue.

When she'd "graduated" from Marstead's linguistics center after going on three years under their tutelage, Marstead had placed her with a "handler" who would be Linnéa's sole Marstead contact, guiding her movements going forward.

Her handler, known to Linnéa simply as Olaf, had informed her that "she" had applied for admittance to a master's program in the Stockholm School of Economics and had been accepted. Olaf had also found Linnéa her own apartment near the campus.

During that first year of school, Linnéa had taken a full load of classes, but she and Olaf also met twice weekly after dark. Linnéa would walk to a nearby car park. Olaf would flash his headlights once, and Linnéa would get into his car. Olaf would then take her to a building Marstead owned where, for two hours or more, Olaf would tutor her on Marstead's business dealings in the Baltic region.

"The Soviet Union is going to collapse, Linnéa," he predicted. "It is only a matter of time before the Communist government fails. And when it does? Marstead must be ready. This incoming U.S. president, Reagan, means business."

Linnéa was skeptical. "But he's just an actor, isn't he?"

"He didn't become president of the Screen Actors Guild and then governor of California for two terms by being 'just' an actor, Linnéa. Watch him. The man is smart. Savvy. And the Soviet Union is ripe for change."

"You are telling me this for a reason, Olaf."

"I am. We are grooming you, Linnéa, investing a great deal of time, money, and effort into you. We expect you to help us make inroads into the USSR after their Communist government falls. We cannot predict what shape the government will take afterward, so we must prepare—*you* must prepare—and be ready to exploit any eventuality."

A portion of Linnéa's preparation, Olaf told her, was to develop a network of international contacts while earning her master's degree. It was why he had enrolled her in the school's International Business program, the program where she was about to start her second year.

The master's degree in International Business was new, the class quite small, no more than two dozen students, only half of whom were Swedish. The other half of the class came from varied points around world—Switzerland, Germany, Great Britain, the U.S., South Korea . . . and, surprising Linnéa, even the Soviet Union. The two Soviet students, a young man and a young woman—cousins, in fact—were the offspring of high-ranking members of the Communist Party.

Olaf had taken an immediate interest in them, had investigated them.

"These privileged scions, the adult children of wealthy Communist oligarchs, are being groomed as the next generation of Party leaders," he pointed out. "Make nice. Get close to them. Develop friendships while avoiding romantic entanglements that might prove problematic later on."

Other students in the program, while polite to the two Communists, wanted little to do with them outside school. Their disdain for the Russian students had been Linnéa's opening.

The master's program had a three-language requirement. Linnéa's first two languages were English and Swedish; her third was Russian. Linnéa had used her facility with Russian to introduce herself.

"I'm Linnéa Olander. *Privyet*." Hello.

"I am Artem Ivanovich Kuznetsov; this is my cousin, Daria."

Linnéa was one or two years older than they were, older than most of her classmates, but the Russians had taken to her. The trio spent time together throughout the academic year, Linnéa gaining their confidence and trust.

Then, as the end of spring semester had neared, the program had required the students to participate in an "International Immersion Field Trip." She and her classmates flew to India and spent two weeks in Bombay observing India's rising entrepreneurship and studying the city's emerging business models. Since the semester officially ended on the last day of the trip, many of the foreign students in the program planned to fly from Bombay directly to their respective homes.

Linnéa finished unpacking, latched her empty suitcase, and sat down on her bed. She put her face in her hands, her thoughts wending down the same path as they had for weeks now.

Bombay. That was where things had begun to go wrong.

"WILL YOU GO HOME to Sweden, Linnéa?" Daria had asked. "Spend your summer with family?"

"No. I will probably spend the summer in my apartment."

"Oh! You had told me before that you have no family left; I apologize for my insensitivity."

Artem overheard Daria's comment. "What? You have no family, Linnéa? None?"

Daria glowered at him. "Did you not hear me apologize for my insensitivity?"

Artem shrugged. "Well, I think you should come with me to my family's summer *dacha*, Linnéa. My mother knows you are my only school friend; she already loves you for it. As she has only two sons, she will pamper you, treat you as the daughter she has always wanted. And my father? He will expedite your visa. You must come home with us."

He pointed at Daria. "Daria's mother is my father's sister. Her family has a *dacha* on the same lake. We are together all summer. You must come; I insist. It will be fun to have you along."

"Yes!" Daria chimed in. "Please come. You could stay with my family in our *dacha*, if you prefer."

Artem frowned. "I asked her first, Daria. She will stay with us."

Linnéa's lips parted to deliver a polite refusal, then closed. "Are these serious invitations? Do you mean it?"

"But of course. A few phone calls, and all will be arranged."

How convenient for you, Linnéa thought—along with the other notions racing around in her mind. "I cannot accept until I make arrangements; I must check with the friend who waters my plants and collects my *Posten* when I am gone."

Artem and Linnéa agreed to go to their rooms and make the long distance calls, then meet up afterward. Linnéa shut the door to the hotel room she shared with Daria, gratified that the girl had gone with Artem instead of following her back to their room. From memory, Linnéa dialed the number to the Marstead employee switchboard.

"Alpha seven three three five," she said when the switchboard operator picked up. She had to wait a full five minutes before her handler picked up.

Glad that's not my dime, she thought while waiting, knowing the long distance charges would be outrageous.

A familiar voice came on the line. "Yes? Aren't you in India?"

"I am, and the trip is scheduled to end in two days. However, I've just received an offer I wished to report to you."

She recounted Artem's invitation—Artem, the second son of Ivan Gregorovich Kuznetsov, one of the most powerful members of the Communist Party in Russia.

"You did well to call this in, Linnéa. Let me consult with my superiors and call you back."

The consultation must have taken a while, because Linnéa didn't receive a call back until late that evening. While Artem had received his parents' immediate and enthusiastic approval to bring Linnéa to Russia, Linnéa had needed to put Artem off until Marstead approved the trip.

"My neighbor wasn't home; I left a message with her daughter to call me back," she said over dinner. "I'll let you know then what she says."

Artem's brows tangled in puzzlement. "You would turn down a summer among the trees with the lake nearby to swim and boat in, over a few potted plants?"

Linnéa laughed. "Maybe not, but I'd like to have both if I can, please. I dearly love my houseplants!"

When her Russians friends laughed with her, she added, "I should also say that I applied for a summer job—just as a helper in the local outdoor market. I have an income from my father's life insurance to see me through school, but I still must supplement it. So, *if* I come, I may only be able to stay a week or two."

Artem exhibited the stubbornness of his privileged upbringing. "If? *If?* Even two weeks in the sun will do you good, Linnéa. You work too hard. You must think of yourself more than you do."

Daria put her hand on Linnéa's "Yes, I agree. Linnéa needs some rest and sunshine—but to tell the truth, she is our *solnyshko*, our little ray of sunshine wherever else she goes, no? I think you are thinking of yourself, Artem. That is why you wish her to come."

Artem grinned. "*Da*. She is our bit of Swedish *solnyshko*—and why I wish her to spend the summer with us."

Linnéa laughed again and had the grace to blush, too. "You two are incorrigible, but I think that's why I love you both."

Late that evening, when Linnéa and Daria were already abed, the phone finally rang.

"That is for me, I wager," Linnéa said cheerfully. With Daria in the room, it would have to be a one-sided conversation.

"Hello? Ah, Lillith. Thank you for calling me back."

Olaf on the other end answered, "I take it you have company in the room?"

"Yes, thank you. So, I called earlier because my friends, Artem and Daria, have invited me to fly home with them for the summer. Actually, I can only spare two weeks if I'm to earn any money before the next term begins. I was wondering if you would continue watering my flowers and collecting my *Posten* for two more weeks?"

"Yes, you are instructed to go, and two weeks is a judicious amount of time. Will Ivan Gregorovich be present during your stay?"

"Uh-huh, I believe so. I'm rather excited about it. Such an unexpected treat!"

Her handler snorted. "Indeed. Well, what we want you to do is nothing. Absolutely *nothing*. You are to do nothing except be your charming, innocent self with the Kuznetsov family, particularly Ivan Gregorovich. We expect you to keep a mental list of everyone you meet, but that is all. Can you do that?"

"But of course."

"Let's see if your relationship with the family progresses. If it does, we'll hope for other opportunities in the future."

"Okay. Thanks, Lillith! See you in a couple weeks."

"Do nothing more than what I said, yes?"

"*Ja*, goodbye." Linnéa hung up and beamed at Daria. "It's all arranged! I think I'm a bit giddy."

IN THE MORNING, she gave Artem the news. "I can come!"

"Good! Then the three of us will fly from here to Moscow tomorrow. Soon after, we will drive to the lake."

"Don't worry if you didn't bring any swimming suits," Daria added, "I have several and will share with you."

Linnéa exchanged her plane ticket to Stockholm for a seat on the same flight as Artem and Daria. They left Bombay early the following day and landed in Moscow at Sheremetyevo Airport quite late.

"You should have been here last year, Linnéa, for the Summer Olympics. It was the grandest spectacle I have ever seen," Artem bragged.

Daria's parents sent a car for them. As they drove through the city, Linnéa observed that all the cars were uniformly black and the pedestrians sported clothing of very little color.

These Muscovites are certainly a dreary lot, she thought.

Then the driver stopped before Artem's family's home, and she was swept inside an apartment of high, gilded ceilings and overstated opulence. Linnéa tried not to gawk.

My word. The perks of the Communist upper crust.

Artem's mother took Linnéa's face in her hands and kissed her on both cheeks. "You are the only classmate in the Swedish school Artem and Daria speak of, Miss Olander. You are most welcome here."

She showed Linnéa to a bedroom twice the size of her own at home with a bed so large that it would not have fit in her room. The driver had already delivered Linnéa's suitcase, and a maid was unpacking for her.

"Come. Come with me. You are hungry, yes? I have a nice dinner waiting for you and Artem. Then you can rest. Day after tomorrow, we go to the lake, to our little *dacha*. My husband will join us there after he returns from his trip abroad."

CHAPTER 15

LINNÉA STEPPED FROM the car and stared at the summer house. What Artem's mother had described over dinner her first night in Moscow as their "little *dacha*" (something akin to a summer cottage), was actually an ornate, two-story wooden structure, a large, well-kept lodge built on a slope, with a wraparound porch, the lake shimmering before it. The dacha's many windows were trimmed in colorfully carved and painted wooden "gingerbread." She noted a detached garage farther up the slope, behind the house, a row of servants' quarters built above it.

The house was surrounded by flowerbeds bursting with blooms that dulled the fact that the lot was enclosed in a high fence of iron bars. Down the slope and through the trees, the sun sparkled on the water. A dock began at the shore and extended many yards out into the lake. A motorboat was moored to the dock. Farther out in the water, she saw an anchored platform, a diving board and a slide built atop it. She turned in a circle; the peaked roofs of two or three other *dachas* were not that far away.

"Daria's family has the *dacha* just there," Artem pointed. "They are to arrive today also."

After a late lunch, Artem walked Linnéa to the lake. "That is our dock and our boat. Would you like to go out in the boat?"

"Yes, please."

"We have a sailing boat, too. They will haul it to the lake tomorrow, now that we are here."

"Oh, I love to sail!"

"Do you know how?"

"Certainly. I am a Swede. I was born to the water."

"Well! Then I shall look forward to sailing with you."

Later that afternoon, a long, sleek car, noticeably larger than the vehicle Artem and Linnéa had arrived in, pulled into the yard. Everyone present at the *dacha*—Artem's mother, Artem, Linnéa, and four servants—gathered in the yard to greet Artem's father as he stepped from his car.

Ivan Kuznetsov was an imposing figure, a large man, not fat or barrel-chested but tall and solidly built. He stood, slowly buttoned his suit jacket, and surveyed his family and servants. Then he walked forward, kissed his wife on both cheeks, and murmured an affectionate greeting. He moved on to Artem.

Artem, the same height as his father but of a thinner build, smiled. "Papa!"

"My son," Ivan replied, kissing him also. "It has been too long."

"I am glad you could come, Papa," Artem said, so obviously proud of his father.

Kuznetsov shifted his eyes to Linnéa. Beneath heavy brows, gray eyes twinkled. "And who is this? Is this your young friend from school for whom I moved half the heavens to procure a visa, Artem?"

"Yes, Papa. May I present Miss Linnéa Olander? She can stay only two weeks with us, but Daria and I are very pleased she is here. Thank you, Papa, for making it possible."

Linnéa offered her hand to him. "*Dobryy den*', sir."

He ignored her hand, grasped her arms near their shoulders, and kissed her on both cheeks. "You are very welcome in my home, Miss Olander. I thank you for being a good friend to Artem and Daria. You will always hold a place in my heart for your kindness to them."

Linnéa was touched. "Th-thank you, sir."

He nodded and passed on, murmuring words of greeting to the household staff. Two bodyguards whose bulging arms made their suits look like they'd been poured into them, followed after Kuznetsov.

"My father likes you, Linnéa," Artem grinned. "This is a good thing."

"What would it look like if he did not like me?" she asked.

He shook his head. "Oh, you would not wish to find out, Linnéa. You must trust my word on this."

DINNER THAT EVENING was at eight, a feast by any stretch of the imagination. The table in the *dacha's* big room, set before an unlit fireplace, was laid in formal fashion, and Daria's family—her, her parents, and a younger brother and sister—were to join them.

"We dress for dinner when Father is here," Artem confided in her. "Daria's mother is tall and slender like you. She is bringing a few dresses for you to choose from."

"Um, okay."

When Daria arrived, she introduced Linnéa to her parents and siblings. Daria and her mother led Linnéa to her room to change for dinner.

"I hope I have brought you something that you would care to wear," Daria's mother, Sofíja said.

Linnéa stared with awe at the three dresses Sofija's maid had laid upon the bed, each a designer original probably costing more than the combined total of everything Linnéa owned. "But they are all quite beautiful. I don't know how to thank you for your kindness."

Sofíja beamed. "Not at all. We are happy you are here."

"I will help you dress," Daria told Linnéa. "We should hurry. Uncle Ivan does not like dinner to be delayed."

Linnéa, with Daria's assistance, slipped into a gauzy blue gown that dropped below her ankles but showed off her bare shoulders and long neck. Linnéa could scarcely believe what she saw in the mirror.

"Oh, Linnéa! You are so beautiful!"

Linnéa laughed. "Thank you, my sweet friend."

When Linnéa and Daria arrived at the dining table, Artem, his father, and his uncle stood. Sofíja nodded her approval and whispered something in Artem's mother's ear that made them chuckle.

"Artem," Ivan said to his son, "Your guest is lovelier than your letters described."

Linnéa blushed. Artem grinned. The rest of the table laughed with good nature. When everyone was seated, Linnéa looked around, feeling welcome and comfortable but also a little puzzled.

What a lovely family, she thought. *Perhaps Russians are not the boogeymen we have thought them to be.*

Artem was looking at her. Everyone was looking at her.

"I beg your pardon?"

Artem said, "Father asked a question of you, Miss Olander."

"Oh! I apologize, Mr. Kuznetsov. I was caught up in my own thoughts." She sighed with a smile. "I was thinking what a lovely family you have and how welcome all of you have made me feel."

Ivan inclined his head. "I am glad you feel comfortable with us, Miss Olander, and I compliment you on your Russian. It is nice to hear it spoken well by a Swede. I was merely asking of your aspirations when you finish your degree?"

"Ah. Thank you; you are most kind. Well, I have a love for technology and scientific innovation, Mr. Kuznetsov. I would like to work on the cutting edge of technology acquisition and transfer, to assist and speed emerging technologies from the laboratory and the test floor to the world marketplace."

It was a rehearsed line, one she had used before, but it did not garner the reaction she had presumed it would. She was surprised and more than a little concerned to see Kuznetsov's brows sink and his eyes narrow and glisten like hard stones.

"I see. A bold aspiration for so lovely a woman." He picked up his wine glass and sipped it, all the while watching her, searching her, speculation glittering in those hard, glinting eyes.

"I'm sorry—have I said something amiss?"

"In Russia, Miss Olander, technology belongs to the state. We who lead the state also guard our emerging technologies. We who lead decide a technology's uses and safeguard its proliferation so that *the state* benefits from it. I have sent Artem and Daria to school in Stockholm so that they will safeguard our technology in the future."

Artem's expression had gone flat. He was carefully addressing his dinner, his chin down. The table had dropped into silent watchfulness.

And everything within Linnéa snapped into its masked mode.

She nodded, thoughtfully, as if reflecting upon Ivan Kuznetsov's words. "Yes. Yes, I see the wisdom and advantages of what you describe, Mr. Kuznetsov."

She lifted her glass to him and added, every word sincere, "Thank you for gifting me with this new perspective—I had not thought of technology in this way, that it should benefit the whole and not the few."

She hesitated and frowned. "It is not what I have been taught." The barest hint of criticism accompanied her last statement, as though she had only realized that she disagreed with her capitalistic instructors.

Kuznetsov sniffed. "They should teach the Communist ways in your Western schools, no?"

"You make another valid point, sir," Linnéa murmured.

The occupants at the table seemed to breathe simultaneously. The tension that had squeezed them as a whole drifted away as quickly as it had risen.

Artem smiled awkwardly, but Linnéa's smile in return was sweet and open, without pretension, full of good will.

"I am having such a lovely time, Artem," she said before them all. "Thank you again for inviting me."

"To Miss Olander," Ivan Kuznetsov ordered, lifting his glass.

The diners raised their glasses and repeated, "To Miss Olander!"

Linnéa blushed and dipped her chin.

Inside, she thought, *Oh, now I see how it is. Dissent at your own peril and risk the ire of a "benevolent" tyrant.*

She slipped a bite of meat into her mouth. *I think our assessment of the Soviets was spot-on after all.*

THEY WERE LYING on the dock, Artem, Daria, and Linnéa, drowsing in the sun after swimming all morning. Linnéa had only the remainder of this day and one more before her flight left Moscow for Stockholm.

"My brother Bogdan comes tomorrow afternoon," Artem murmured. "He is bringing a friend with him. It is too bad you are leaving so soon after they arrive. We would have had such good times! Are you certain you can stay no longer?"

"There's no telephone here, Artem, and I have changed my plans once already. I must go home and earn some money."

"Isn't your tuition paid for by the state?" Artem could become querulous quite easily.

"Yes, and if I don't squander the little that is left of my father's life insurance, I will have enough to buy books and pay my rent through next June."

"See? You have plenty. You do not need to go home to work in a common street market."

"I also care to eat occasionally," was Linnéa's dry response.

"Leave her alone, Artem," Daria ordered. "Our parents give us everything. She has no one. Let her be."

Linnéa blinked. *She has no one. Let her be.* After close to four years in Sweden, how accurately that described how she felt. *Increasingly alone. With no one.*

What did you expect while learning and practicing deception? that old voice whispered. *That you would find happiness? For you?*

She turned over, but the voice, once started, would not shut up.

She climbed to her feet. "One more dip! First one to the platform wins!"

She was halfway across the water to the diving platform before Artem and Daria reacted.

"LINNÉA, THIS IS MY brother, Bogdan. Bogdan, may I present Miss Olander, our friend from school?"

Linnéa greeted Artem's brother, whom she decided was in his late twenties but who already wore the weight of his responsibilities on his creased brow and in the shadows hanging beneath his eyes.

"A pleasure to meet you, Bogdan."

"As it is to meet you, Miss Olander. May I introduce my dear friend, Pyotr?"

"Pyotr Sergeyevich Anosov, at your service, Miss Olander."

A shaft of lightning, sizzling hot, then icy cold, pierced Linnéa's chest. She clenched her teeth to keep her smile intact, to maintain control over her reaction, her expression. Shifting her gaze from Bogdan to his friend, she saw first the square superhero jaw, then the jet-black hair above.

She lifted her hand. "Linnéa Olander. A pleasure to meet you, Pyotr."

She couldn't look in his amber eyes as he shook her hand. Instead she passed over them and concentrated above, on his forehead, blocking everything else out. Her vision had tunneled, leaving the edges blurry. Darkened. She allowed only what she chose to see to enter that narrow field of focus.

"Sadly, Miss Olander could only stay two weeks with us, and her plane leaves tomorrow," Artem explained. "She and our driver must leave for the city before breakfast to make her flight."

"That is indeed regrettable—don't you agree, Pyotr?"

"Very much so. I should have liked to know you better, Miss Olander. You are Swedish, are you not?"

"Yes, I am." She turned away, toward Artem and Bogdan.

Bogdan said a few more things that Linnéa responded to; his friend stayed silent.

Why are you here? Linnéa kept asking herself. *How in the world could we have run into each other—and here of all places?*

Artem took Linnéa's arm and gently tugged on it. "Linnéa, it is past time for lunch, and you must be starved—you are looking a bit peaked, I think."

Linnéa grabbed on to his suggestion. "Thank you. I am famished."

SHE LEFT THE following morning, managing to avoid encountering Bogdan's friend again. She boarded her flight at a quarter to ten and arrived in Stockholm at half past noon. Before she collected her luggage, she found her way to the closest pay phone.

She called the Marstead employee line, collect.

"Alpha seven three three five."

"One moment, please."

As usual, a Marstead "moment" was minutes. "Yes?"

"I've arrived home; I'm still at the airport."

"Yes? Do you have something to report?"

"The names of those I met lest I forget anything."

Olaf chided her. "It couldn't have waited for us to meet face to face? Or is something wrong?"

"I wanted to report sooner than that, and a pay phone at the airport is safer than one on the street. Let me . . . let me list the names, please." From memory, she recited the name of every individual, even the Kuznetsov's servants, in the order in which she'd encountered them.

She reached the end of her list with, "Bodgan Kuznetsov and his friend, Pyotr Sergeyevich Anosov."

Olaf sucked in his breath. "Pyotr Anosov. You're certain?"

"Yes."

Her handler spoke more to himself than to her. "Well, that was unexpected." To Linnéa he replied, "What about him?"

"I . . . I was in training with him. Four years ago."

"Ah. I see now why you were anxious to report. Did it shake you? Did either of you give an indication that you knew the other?"

"No, and we didn't speak after introductions."

"Very good, Linnéa. It is uncommon but not unheard of to meet an operative we knew . . . from before. Thank you for calling it in. I understood him to be in Moscow, but I'll check with his handler to ensure that all is well."

"He . . . perhaps he came to Ivan Kuznetsov's *dacha* for the same reasons I did. To observe Kuznetsov."

"Yes, very likely."

LINNÉA SAT UP AND wiped the fatigue from her face. The chance encounter with Black had shaken her and, in the weeks since then, even while home on leave, she hadn't been able to let it go.

If only Artem's brother had come a day later.

If only I hadn't accepted Artem's invitation!

But she had. And when Bogdan had introduced his friend and the familiar voice had reached her, stunned her? When she'd seen the same astonishment ripple over Black's face—even if the other observers had not noticed? In that instant, shock *and desire* had resonated from him to her. Like an invisible tidal wave, longing had surged from him, had crashed into her . . . and she'd been undone.

A fire ignited between them that, even now, Linnéa could not escape: It pulsed within her, a crazed, hot yearning. While she'd been Laynie, while she'd been in America with her parents and Sammie, the need had cooled somewhat. But the moment she'd reached London and become Linnéa again, her desire had reignited. From London to Stockholm, it pummeled her, demanded what she could not have. It clawed at her—a craving, incessant hunger.

I must get a grip on myself, on my emotions, on my body.

I must.

ALTHOUGH SHE WAS TIRED from the long transition back to Sweden, Linnéa found it difficult to fall asleep. When her worn body succumbed at last to its needed rest, she tossed fitfully, her dreams troubled.

In them, Black whispered her name: *Mags. Maggie. Sweet Maggie.* His gentle fingertips stroked her cheek . . .

Linnéa woke with a start. A dark figure sat beside her on the edge of the bed.

"Maggie."

She gasped and shuddered. "Black?"

"Shhhh," he soothed her. "Yes. It's me."

"How? What are you doing here?"

"Could I stay away after seeing you again, after learning who and where you were? A few weeks after we met, I left Russia for my 'annual leave.' The moment I set foot on American soil, I turned around and came back, but you weren't here."

"But how did you find me?"

"I searched Artem's room at the *dacha*; he had you in his address book. Then, when I arrived in Stockholm and you weren't here, I realized you were likely home on leave, too. So, I have been in Stockholm, for weeks, waiting for you to return."

Linnéa reached for the lamp at the side of her bed. His hand closed around hers.

"No lights, please. That would not be wise."

"But I want to see you."

"I want to see you, too, but I want to hold you more."

They fell into each other's arms, touching, embracing, murmuring their desires and longings.

"Oh, Mags! I have been only half a man since we parted at the airport in Baltimore. When I saw you again, my heart nearly burst for joy."

She could only weep—weep for the ache that his presence soothed, the emptiness he filled. Arms entwined, they lay back on her bed.

They came together in the dark.

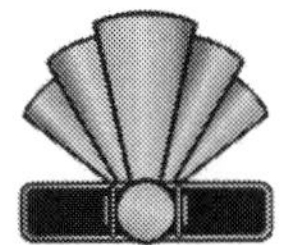

CHAPTER 16

THEY REMAINED SEQUESTERED in Linnéa's apartment for two days. Two days of bliss, of shutting out the world around them, of ignoring every distraction. They allowed nothing to disturb or separate them.

Neither of them were unrealistic; they knew their situation was and could only be transitory but, by tacit agreement, they didn't speak of what came next—not until the evening of the second day approached, when Linnéa was scheduled to meet with Olaf and receive her next assignment.

Her head bowed, Linnéa told him what he already knew. "If I don't go, if I miss our rendezvous, he will come looking for me."

"I understand."

"And you? When are you scheduled to transition from the States back to your assignment?"

His chin—that dear, sharp, jutting chin!—touched his chest. "The day before yesterday."

"Oh, no . . ."

Marstead will not forgive him this infraction. He will be ruined.

Trammel's warnings and whole passages from the NDAs they had signed rushed to the forefront of her thoughts.

If we break the terms of this nondisclosure agreement, we can be brought up on charges in a closed, secret court and serve a prison term outside American jurisdiction?

He may as well have read her mind. "It was worth it, Maggie. I would do it again."

And me? Would I risk everything for you? For our love?

She found that she was uncertain. She already ached with loss, but would she give up her place with Marstead for Black? Could she? Was the exchange worth what it would cost?

"What . . . what will you do?"

"Wait here for them to come get me."

But, oh, my love! They will never let us see each other again, no matter what either of us does . . . you know that. And if I do not tell them where you are?

"Then hold me, Black. Hold me until they come. Please don't let go."

JUST AFTER DARKNESS had fallen, Linnéa left her apartment and walked the half-mile to the car park to meet Olaf. He was waiting for her and flashed his headlights. When she climbed into his car, he did not start the engine. Instead, he gripped the steering wheel and came directly to the point.

"The day before yesterday, Pyotr Anosov did not return from his annual leave as scheduled. Our superiors are quite concerned about this breach of protocol. You reported meeting him at Kuznetsov's *dacha* in June. I need to know if you have heard from him since that time. Have you? Tell me, Linnéa."

He didn't want her to be involved, did not want to believe the worst. She looked in his face and saw a flicker of hope there.

She crushed it.

"He was waiting for me when I returned from the States. We have been together since then."

Angry blood flooded up Olaf's neck. "Are you out of your *blanking* mind, Linnéa? Marstead will drop you from the program; you'll be lucky if you don't end up in some moldy cell somewhere until Marstead's NATO partners are satisfied that you haven't compromised us or collaborated against us! We will have lost *everything* we have invested in you—not to mention the hopes we had for your future service."

She lifted one shoulder. "He is waiting for you; he won't give you any trouble." Sighing, sensing but putting down a quiver of uneasiness, she added, "He simply showed up. I didn't know he was coming. How could I?"

Olaf studied her. "It's not for me to decide your future. Right now? I need to call this in."

"I understand." She opened the door to climb out.

"No. You stay with me until this is resolved."

Linnéa turned and smiled sadly. "I'll be at my apartment, Olaf. Whomever they send, they need not fear that either of us will run; we will cooperate."

"Linnéa!"

She ignored him and walked away.

A block from her apartment, the uneasy feeling she'd been snubbing grew to an alarm she could not ignore. She ran the last block, pounded up the steps, unlocked the door, and threw it open.

"Black! Black, where are you?"

An empty echo answered her.

She found the note on her night table.

Maggie,

I couldn't bear to ruin your life along with mine. As soon as you left, I called to turn myself in. We arranged a pickup location, and I am leaving for it now. Don't follow me, please.

It wasn't fair of me to put you in jeopardy. I will take responsibility for my actions and not implicate you but, as I told you earlier, it was worth it to me. If we never meet again—and I doubt we will—it was still worth it to hold you once, to know that what I felt when we parted, four years ago, wasn't all in my mind, that you did love me, as I have loved you, all this time.

Take care of yourself, Mags; I will never forget you.

Black

"No! Oh, no, Black, no! Oh, I wanted . . . I needed to kiss you one last time." She sank to the floor, sobbing, pressing the note to her breasts, covering it with her tears.

WHEN THE EXPECTED knock sounded on her door, Linnéa sighed. She had destroyed Black's note, tearing it to tiny pieces and flushing it away. She had washed her face and tidied herself. She walked to the door and looked through the peephole.

Olaf.

My fate hinges on these next minutes.

She opened the door and he entered. He stood just inside her tiny apartment, hands on his hips, jaw working.

"What is it, Olaf?"

He glanced at her, then down at his feet. "By the time I reached out to my superiors to tell them that I knew where Pyotr was, he had already called them and made arrangements to give himself up. I didn't get a chance to tell them what you and I discussed; they were on their way to get him and were too busy to listen to me. I understand they picked him up forty-five minutes ago."

Linnéa nodded, waiting for the hammer to fall.

It did not.

"Somehow or other, you have not been implicated in Pyotr's 'indiscretions'—not yet anyway."

Linnéa's thoughts were racing ahead, ordering themselves, determining a new way forward. "What . . . what will happen to him?"

"That depends. Depends on whether they find any activities that compromised him, his identity, mission, or the network. Depends upon the excuses he comes up with."

He glanced up. "*Your* status depends on whether he brings you into it—although I cannot believe that Marstead knows nothing of your relationship with him. How long has it been going on, anyway?"

She lifted her chin. "Going on? I don't know what you mean. I . . . I haven't seen or communicated with this man since training. Not until we met quite by coincidence at Ivan Kuznetsov's *dacha*. I hardly know him other than that."

"But he broke with protocol and left his U.S. identity during annual leave to come here to Stockholm. To see you."

Linnéa blinked slowly, her eyes never leaving Olaf's. "To see me? No, I don't think so. Why would he be interested in me? As I said, I haven't seen that man since our chance encounter in Russia."

Olaf's chin jerked up. "You haven't seen him since your chance encounter in Russia?"

"Well, of course not. And that was back in June—I reported it to you the moment I arrived from Russia to Stockholm, remember? Called you from the airport? Marstead must know where Pyotr was after I ran into him, before he left for his leave in the States, before he came to Sweden, yes? So, they certainly know he wasn't here with me during that time."

She shrugged, growing a bit irritated. "I have no idea why this man broke protocol or why he chose to come to Stockholm, but I only returned from my own month of annual leave three days ago—so how could he have been with me? I have been busy prepping for my classes to start next week."

"But you told me—" He stared at her, taken aback, then dumbfounded, before he snorted the softest of laughs.

Once, then twice, he chuckled to himself.

Looking away and shaking his head, he murmured, "Bravo, Linnéa. Well played."

CHAPTER 17

LINNÉA ACCEPTED THAT she would never see Black again, but she let herself relive their two nights and two days together. It was the solitary consolation prize she permitted herself to feast on . . . for a time.

Winter came with November; then it was Christmas. School closed, and her friends—including Artem and Daria—went home for the holidays. Living so far from her family made Christmas the loneliest time of Linnéa's year. The Russian cousins invited, then begged and wheedled, for her to come with them for Christmas. She refused, to Artem's great disgust.

No, she needed to call home on Christmas, as she had since moving to Sweden, and doing so from Moscow would not have been possible.

Christmas morning was like any other morning, except for opening the present Mama, Dad, and Sam had sent. She saved her phone call until late Christmas evening: It was the bright spot to look forward to in an otherwise dull day.

She didn't call from her apartment—that was not allowed. In fact, she had led her parents to believe she didn't have a phone.

Instead, whenever she called them, she used the pay phone inside an all-night diner near the school. The diner was owned by an Asian family, the Chows. Since they didn't celebrate Christmas or close their restaurant on Christmas Day, she rode her bike through the quiet, cold night to their restaurant, splurging on a late Christmas dinner. At 8 p.m. in Stockholm, it would be eleven in the morning in Seattle, and Mama, Dad, and Sam would have opened their gifts and finished breakfast.

"Thanks for the cool sweater, sis," Sam said. He'd grabbed the phone first—he always did on Christmas. "The note inside said you bought it from a Swedish woman who carded and spun the wool herself, then knit it? I'm impressed. And it fits great, too!"

"I gave Inga your measurements. She is seventy-eight, I think, still going strong. She has a booth in the street market near my apartment. Her son raises the sheep and provides her with the wool. Everything about her work is authentic and traditional Swedish, including the pattern knit into your sweater. When I raved over her work, she said she would knit whatever I liked for you."

"Well, gotta say I love it. Powdery gray, navy, and cream are cool, masculine colors."

She smiled. "Wouldn't send you anything less than 'masculine,' bro. Please send me a photo? I'd like to show it to Inga. She'd like that a lot."

She laughed. "Oh! Speaking of pictures, thank *you* for the camera. I know the three of you went together to buy it, and I'm so excited to try it out."

They chattered for a while, then Sam said, "Hey, Dad needs to talk to you, too."

Needs to talk to me?

It seemed an odd transition.

"Okay, Sam. I love you. Take care."

"Love you, too, sis."

"Hi there, Little Duck. Merry Christmas!"

"Dad! It's so good to hear your voice. I miss all of you terribly on Christmas morning."

"Well, we miss you, too, Laynie. Say, there's something I need to talk to you about."

There it was again.

He was moving, taking the phone into the kitchen and closing the swinging door behind him, and she was suddenly afraid.

"What is it, Dad?"

"Well, Laynie-girl, there isn't an easy way to say this. You remember when you were home last summer and we talked about Mama being a little slow and unsteady on her feet? That we got her a doctor's appointment in October?"

Fear uncoiled like a serpent in her belly. She slumped against the wall next to the pay phone.

"Wh-what is it, Dad?"

"Her doctor ran some tests, then sent her to a specialist who did even more tests. Took them a few weeks to get all the results, to be certain of their diagnosis, but they are now, honey.

“Mama has MS. Multiple sclerosis. You know what that is?”

“Sort of. Not really.”

“It’s a degenerative disease, Laynie. It can be slow or fast, but it will worsen over time.”

“I . . .” She didn’t know what to say. The prospect of her mama in a wheelchair or dying had choked off her words, her thoughts. Polly wasn’t old! Fifty-eight wasn’t old!

“Mama has a walker now, to help her stand and get around when her legs are weak. We’ve got her a doctor who specializes in MS, too. He has some drugs for her to try, says they will help slow the disease’s progression. Other than that, nothing’s changed.”

“But . . .” She had so many questions and could put none of them into words.

“Nothing’s changed, Laynie. She’s not going to die, not anytime soon and, with help, she can live a happy, productive life for many years to come. I have a few years until retirement, but should I need to retire early to take care of her, I will.”

“Should I . . . should I come home?”

“And leave your master’s degree unfinished? Not on your life, Little Duck. Don’t you worry now. We’re fine. Mama’s fine. Stephen’s close by if we need him.”

She heard him take the phone back into the dining room. “Here’s Mama now. She wants to talk to you.”

“Hey, Mama!” Her throat was tight, her words overly bright.

“Dad give you the news, did he? I tol’ him not to on Christmas, that it would ruin your day, but he says talking on the telephone is better than a letter, and we can’t call you ourselves since you don’ have a phone.”

“I’m sorry, Mama.”

I’m sorry for what you’re facing. Sorry I’m not there. Sorry I lie to you. Sorry I’ve let you down, Mama.

“Sorry? For what, sugar? You’re growed up now. We raised you to be strong, to dream, to do great things with your life. You doin’ all that, an’ we’re so proud of you.”

She sobbed softly, her face to the wall, hand over the receiver.

“Laynie? Laynie-girl? You crying? Baby, you stop that right now. We-all are fine. My mind is clear and strong; only my legs are a bit wobbly is all. You focus on your schoolin’, hear? You hear me?”

She croaked out a, “Yes, Mama.”

“’Sides, my Jesus? He’s a-holdin’ me, Laynie. Liftin’ me up on eagles’ wings, he is. He knows ever’ hair on m’ head and knows the length of m’ days. When I go home to him—someday far in the future, Lord willin’, there’ll be no more tears, no more pain, no more sorrow. I put all m’ hope in him.”

Polly cleared her throat. “Now, I’m finished with that. Let’s talk about something nice.”

“Yes, Mama.”

When they hung up, Linnéa sank to the floor next to the phone box, buried her head in her arms, and wept. When Mrs. Chow’s head appeared from around the corner, concern wrinkling her face, Linnéa sniffed, wiped her face on her sleeves, and got up.

“I’m fine, Mrs. Chow. Have a nice evening, all right?”

CHAPTER 18

LP

February 1982

LINNÉA LOOKED FOR OLAF in the parking garage. Winter in Stockholm could be frigid, especially when the incoming wind blew over the water, picking up moisture. When Olaf flashed his headlights, Linnéa walked quickly to his car and got in, glad for the vehicle's roaring heater.

He waited until they'd left the garage behind, then he spoke. "Something important has come up, Linnéa, so pay attention. We have a visitor waiting for us at our normal meeting place. His name is Lars Alvarsson, the man who runs Marstead's Stockholm office. He has a job for you—and it's going to be tricky."

Linnéa nodded. "All right." She was impressed: Lars Alvarsson was an important man in Marstead's public hierarchy.

"I have been authorized to tell you that, although you won't finish your master's program until June, this op is something of a 'final' exam for your probationary status. If Alvarsson approves of how you handle yourself and how you complete the assignment, you'll be assigned to him and his office. The big leagues, Linnéa."

At last!

"What do I need to do?"

"He'll fill you in, but I should caution you again—the task is an important one."

They didn't speak further until they arrived at their usual meeting place. Once inside, Linnéa saw that Alvarsson was waiting for them.

He rose from the table where he was sitting. "Miss Olander? Lars Alvarsson."

"Good to meet you, sir."

"Please sit down, Miss Olander."

Alvarsson wasn't that old, perhaps in his early forties. He was a native Swede, Linnéa thought, with the dirty blonde hair and soft blue eyes of someone who descended from pure Scandinavian stock. He was dressed casually, but Linnéa caught a whiff of discomfort.

Accustomed to wearing a suit and tie, are you?

"Has Olaf told you why we're meeting, Miss Olander?"

"Please feel free to call me Linnéa, sir. He has only said that you have a task for me, something delicate."

She was calm and succinct and withstood his inspection with indifference.

She is also lovelier than the photographs Olaf showed me, he thought.

"It *is* delicate and must be handled with finesse. One of our agents, fairly new in the field, was in a Hamburg bar six months ago when a stranger struck up a conversation. We understand that they soon became fast friends and drinking buddies, although we have yet to put eyes on this man. However, in the past three months, we've suffered a series of losses that we believe tie directly to this relationship."

He coughed as cover while seeking for the right words. "We think our man has gotten himself entangled with the East Germans."

Linnéa, for her part, studied Alvarsson and wondered at his discomfort. If the situation were as simple as, "Our man has gotten himself entangled with the East Germans," why hadn't they just pulled the agent out?

What is he not telling me?

She didn't speak; she simply waited.

Alvarsson, on the other hand, wished she *would* say something. He wanted her to ask him the questions she had to be asking of herself, anything that might make it easier for him to ease into what they needed her to do. Having himself spent ten years in the field, Alvarsson realized he had lacked at the end of his field experience the poise that this fledgling already possessed and seemed to own naturally. To some degree, he was annoyed; more galling, he found himself admiring her.

Finally, he spit out what had to be said. "The problem, Miss Olander, is that we believe the East German agent is also one of ours—and, to date, we haven't been able to identify who it is."

There it was: the real problem.

Linnéa asked, "A Stasi agent has infiltrated Marstead? Or the Stasi has turned one of ours?"

The Stasi, the *Ministerium für Staatssicherheit*, was the state security service of the German Democratic Republic (AKA, East Germany, a socialist nation and a satellite state of the Soviet Union).

In Linnéa's tradecraft training, Chin had described the Stasi—headed by the infamous Erich Mielke—as one of the most effective and brutal intelligence agencies in the world, rivaling even the KGB at its apex.

"We don't know which. Obviously, if one of theirs has infiltrated Marstead, that poses the gravest threat but, at present, we have only suppositions."

"You considered having our operative set up this Stasi man but rejected that approach. Why?"

Alvarsson's eyes narrowed. "Our man is compromised, and his career with us is done—whether he was a willing or an unwitting, duped accomplice. So, whichever way this ends? It won't end well for him. Not exactly motivation for him to help us."

"*. . . You can expect us—and we promise—to rain hellfire down upon you and yours.*"

"I understand, sir. What are your orders?"

"Our primary objective is to identify and capture the double agent, preferably alive, so that we can question him and ascertain how deep the damage goes, after which we take our man into custody, too."

"And if the primary objective can't be managed?"

Alvarsson lifted his chin. "You'll need to take him out."

Linnéa sank into her training, letting it take and guide her, walling off emotional responses. "Yes, sir."

Then, "Why me, sir?"

Alvarsson nodded slowly. "You deserve to know. For one, you are young and unknown in the field. That means neither our man nor the traitor will know you. For another, Olaf here tells me you are the brightest young operative he has brought up in a decade, that you think on your feet, that you are up to this job."

He leaned across the table, his eyes boring into hers. "If he is wrong, tell me now."

Linnéa, her gaze unwavering, answered, "I can do what you are asking, sir."

Alvarsson sat back. "Very well, then. Let's go over the operational plans." He placed a photograph on the table. "This is our man, Gerold Weiß. He is known to frequent a Hamburg bar called the *Wilder Krieger* in the *Speicherstadt* warehouse district. This is where he meets the traitor."

"What can you tell me about Weiß?"

"He is accustomed to the trappings of wealth and moves easily in monied circles. The nightlife of *Wilder Krieger* is precisely what he prefers. We will put you into the country under a solid cover. You'll go to that bar and attract our man. We'll have two teams on the ground to support you, but the initial work—that of cozying up to Weiß, then sticking around to ID the double agent—will be yours."

Alvarsson coughed to clear his throat, that same sign of discomfort Linnéa had noted earlier.

"We think the best way to exit the bar with both men in tow is on the pretext of a *ménage à trois*. Suggest taking them to your hotel room. Our people will be watching the bar's exits. They will alert the next team to follow you, and they will follow the team following you. Our operatives will take them both at the earliest possible opportunity.

"I am sending you to a clothier, one of ours. Olaf will drive you to her as soon we finish here. She will outfit you with attire, uh, suitable for cruising the *Wilder Krieger*."

Linnéa nodded.

I'm to be the bait on the hook. Can I do this?

I think so.

But can you kill a man if you need to?

She shuddered inside.

It might be easier than playing a whore.

Alvarsson gestured to Olaf. Olaf placed a compact semiauto and a thigh holster on the table between Alvarsson and Linnéa. He added a second magazine.

Laynie glanced at the weapon. *Beretta, .32 ACP. 3.5 inch barrel. Fairly light, but a tricky safety.*

She scooped them into her handbag.

"Olaf will finish briefing you, Miss Olander. You leave for Hamburg tomorrow."

OLAF TOOK LINNÉA to Marstead's clothier. Two hours later, Olaf piled seven shopping bags containing evening gowns, undergarments, shoes, and accessories into his back seat.

On the drive back to the parking garage, Linnéa was quiet. *I'll be a tart but a well-dressed, high-end one*, her sardonic humor commented.

When Olaf pulled in to let her out, she didn't move. She was still deep in her own considerations.

Finally, she asked, “Olaf, are you carrying?”

He glanced over, concerned. “Why do you ask?”

“I want a backup piece. Something even smaller than the Beretta.”

He grunted. “I saw those dresses you’ll be wearing. Where on God’s green earth would you put it?”

He was right; she planned to carry the Beretta in her fancy clutch for that very reason, because nothing she would be wearing in Hamburg stood a chance of concealing a gun, even one smaller than the Beretta, except in a thigh holster. And Linnéa could not risk Gerold Weiß’s roaming fingers coming upon it.

“I’ll come up with something,” she answered.

CHAPTER 19

"PULL OVER TO THAT corner, please," she asked the cabby in passable German. When he stopped, she opened the cab's rear door. Around her, music pulsed from various bars and nightclubs and the shouts and laughter of partiers and boisterous bar hoppers reverberated in the street.

Arranging a silver fox stole about her shoulders, she levered a long, stockinged leg from the cab to the street and placed a sparkling-red, three-inch heel on the pavement. She pivoted her foot a little to the side to flex her calf muscle, ensuring that, as she stood, the slit in her dress split open like a crimson curtain all the way up her sleek thigh—thus guaranteeing that the eyes of every watcher would be glued to her.

They were.

With a casual toss of her upswept hair, Petra Nilsson freed a few dangling curls caught in the fur wrap and stepped onto the sidewalk and into Hamburg's bustling, sordid nightlife.

A glitzy red evening bag clutched in one hand, she twined her arms loosely within the stole. That allowed the fur panels to hang from the crooks of her elbows and the wrap to swoop below her bare back. The stole draped over the curves of her hips and derrière, undulating like a living thing with every languid step.

In the cold evening air, the shimmering stole did absolutely nothing to warm her, and that was just fine. To onlookers, she was already lit from within, a walking furnace of sensuality.

Down the sidewalk she strode, toward her destination, the *Wilder Krieger*—the Wild Warrior—rumored to be "the place" where men and women of certain means and appetites gathered to play. Men passing her from the opposite direction turned to stare; women nudged each other. Catcalls and whistles followed her, but Petra's lofty serenity never altered.

The doormen at the entrance to the bar saw her coming, glanced at each other, and cleared a path for her to the front of the line.

"*Mein Himmel*," a man whispered behind her back.

Petra did not linger inside the entrance; she made her way directly to the middle of the glossy-black bar where she ordered a brandy. When she received the snifter, she turned her back to the bar, put the glass to her lips, and surveyed the room.

Half the men were looking back, but she made eye contact with none of them. She had Gerold Weiß's image on a mental poster while she scanned the room and made like she was sipping her brandy.

"May I buy you a drink?" The man had appeared at her elbow as if by magic.

Petra smiled seductively. "I am waiting for someone in particular . . . but if he doesn't show?" She let the suggestion hang.

The man bowed. "I must hope he is unavoidably detained!"

Petra laughed softly and turned away—only to spot Gerold Weiß himself at a table perhaps twenty feet away.

"Hello," she whispered low in her throat.

He could not possibly have heard her, but he glanced up anyway.

His eyes widened. Petra's welcoming smile caused him to shiver with happy anticipation. He came to her immediately. Petra shifted her body toward him, knowing his gaze would fall to her bare bosom.

It did.

"My word—you stand out in this room like a beacon," he gushed. "There isn't another woman here who holds a candle to you."

"Perhaps I wanted to ensure that the right man saw me."

He held out his hand. "Gerold Weiß. I hope and pray I am the right man."

"Petra," she purred. "I apologize that my German is not as good as yours. I'm Swedish."

"Not at all! Come, Petra; I have a table. I would love to know you better."

She allowed him to draw her along after him, passing the man who'd offered to buy her a drink and who raised his glass to her with a woebegone expression.

Once seated, they made light conversation, the polite exchange of surface information.

"Petra, what brings you to Hamburg?"

"Business, of course. I am a bored accountant by day . . . and a wild, passionate woman by night. I heard this place was the right place to find men who are also . . . wild and passionate."

Weiß's pinkening complexion told Petra that he was excited. "You've certainly gotten my attention."

Petra sipped her brandy, merely wetting her mouth with it. Her sultry glance scorched him, then passed on to look around the bar. "Good; I am so glad to hear it. Perhaps we could go to my hotel? All we need is . . . a friend. Another man. I am a little picky, though. Surely you have someone suitable in mind?"

The pupils of Weiß's eyes flared. "I do, indeed! You will like him—he can be quite droll at times, but he is a man of exceptional taste with an eye for quality; however, I am to meet him elsewhere . . ." he looked at his watch, "in about twenty minutes."

Petra sighed and leaned toward Weiß. "How troublesome . . . unless we could meet him together? Is it another bar?"

"No, it is . . ." He frowned, considering something, then brightened. "It does not matter, my dove. Come with me—that is, if you will be warm enough?"

"Why, where are we going?"

"I am to meet him on the Brooksbrücke, a bridge over the Binnenhafen, about a ten-minute walk from here."

"We could take a taxi, no?" She smiled and drew her stole over her bare shoulders. "I didn't exactly come dressed for winter pastimes."

"You certainly did not!" He laughed; it was an easy, relaxed laugh, and Petra laughed with him.

"All right, then. A taxi it is. And when we reach the bridge, you can remain in the warm cab while I . . . . tell him about our plans for the evening."

Weiß signaled the maître d' and had him call them a cab. While they waited, he lifted her hand and stroked it. "Ah, Petra . . . what a lovely woman you are."

"Oh, no. I assure you, I am not a lovely woman, but an outrageous one, as I intimated."

It was all she could do at this point to keep the pretense going, but she had to push, keep edging him a little further, lest his better judgement prevail.

When the cab arrived, a delicate, frosty fog had descended on the night. Weiß began to issue the driver turn-by-turn instructions—but not, at first blush, for any destination a meagre ten-minute walk from the club. The driver, throwing a dubious look over his shoulder, drove a circuitous route through the warehouse district as Weiß directed him.

Petra tried to keep track of where they were, but as the fog increased, even the street signs were swaddled in it. They twice turned down alleyways, and where they emerged, Petra could not tell. The cabby, however, under Weiß's guidance, eventually delivered them to their destination.

The bridge and the water beneath it were shrouded in mist; the frosty particles suspended in the air muted the many lights around them, enclosing them in a hazy web.

Weiß got out. "Wait here," he ordered the driver. "I'll return shortly."

Petra scanned around, but saw no sign of the team that was supposed to follow them. She reassured herself with, *If they are that good, I shouldn't be able to spot them.*

Weiß started across the bridge, the mist swirling about him, clearing away a little with the breeze. He had reached the center of the bridge when a small car, on its way across, slowed, then stopped. A figure got out and joined Weiß.

They talked. Petra thought the stranger shook his head. She saw Weiß gesture with his hand and point toward the cab. The stranger again shook his head. Weiß appeared to be pleading with him.

Petra's heartbeat quickened. *The traitor doesn't like the idea. Perhaps he smells the trap.*

But minutes later, Weiß returned and paid the cabby. "Come, Petra. We will go to your hotel in his car."

"Your friend appears reluctant."

Weiß shrugged. "He prefers not to mix business with pleasure. However, when I described you, he made an exception."

"I said I was selective," she sniffed, stalling for time. She still hadn't caught sight of their Marstead tail and was growing concerned.

"Do not worry, Petra; my friend has suggested that we return to the club, have a drink, and give you opportunity to take his measure. I promise you will approve of him. If, however, you do not, you may decide then how you wish to proceed. Come. Let's get you into his warm car."

The bridge was not a long structure, but the fog, now falling in tiny, icy bits, obscured its far end, the arching girders disappearing into the shimmering haze. As they drew closer to the center, Petra saw that the roadway was just broad enough for a car to pull to the side, compelling the light traffic to flow around it.

Petra wrapped her stole about her against the wet chill, and she grasped her pocketbook beneath the furs, one hand fingering the flap of the pocketbook's side pouch. The man, who'd had his back to them, turned as they approached.

"Good evening," he drawled. "Petter Eklund at your—"

His greeting hitched—and he produced a small cough to cover his blunder. Nicely done though it was, she knew he was startled.

Dumbfounded.

As dismayed as she was.

Was it a flicker of regret that flashed from his eyes to hers?

Then he recovered himself and sketched a light bow. "At your service," he finished, smiling at her. Confident. Unshaken.

Well, wasn't that how they had been trained to respond should they encounter another agent in the field, someone they knew "from before"?

Weiß spoke next, "Miss Nilsson is not dressed for the out-of-doors; shall we go somewhere warmer to get acquainted as you suggested?"

Eklund inclined his head in agreement and reached for the handle on the car door, but Linnéa had already drawn the Beretta. She leveled it at him and backed to a safe distance.

"Step back from the vehicle, Taylor. Over to the railing."

Taylor. Her gorge rose; she felt nauseous. Sick.

Weiß stared at Linnéa. "What the **blank**? What is going on?"

"Get over there with him," she ordered. She used her free hand to wave him toward the railing of the bridge, but she didn't allow her gun hand to shift even a fraction from Taylor.

"He's working for the Stasi, Weiß, did you know? He's a traitor. The question is, are you?"

Weiß looked from her to Eklund, first in confusion, then in horror as understanding dawned. "No! I'm no traitor! We had orders. He . . ." he pointed at Taylor but spoke to Linnéa, "he showed me our orders, encrypted orders. We were working an op together to *penetrate* the Stasi. He had turned one of their operatives, and we were feeding him doctored intel. Disinformation."

Linnéa sneered at how quickly Weiß had shed his cover to protest his innocence, but she kept her focus on Taylor.

"Not disinformation, Weiß. Real intel. You and he have been feeding the East Germans authentic, actionable intelligence. Where do you suppose that leaves you?"

"But I didn't know! I-I . . ." His mouth worked. "I swear to you, I didn't know. Whatever the Company asks me to do to prove it, I'll do it."

"I'm sure you'll get your chance."

Taylor hadn't moved or changed his expression, so Linnéa couldn't watch him sort through his options, but she didn't need to. With Weiß already testifying against him, coupled with the fact that Marstead had enough evidence on him to send an agent undercover to smoke him out, Taylor had to know that he wouldn't be talking his way out of the trouble he was in.

. . . we promise to rain hellfire down upon you and yours.

Oh, Taylor!

Her old friend lifted one shoulder and smiled that lazy smile she would never forget. "Certainly, we had orders—orders I fabricated. Quite a good forgery, in fact, I'd say. And it wasn't personal, Weiß. I just like the money."

Linnéa's gun hand shook with disbelief. Rage. "Money? You sold us out for *money?*"

He shrugged again. "I didn't betray Marstead's secrets or network—how could I have done so, given their rabid culture of 'anonymity'? I simply sold information to the highest bidder."

He laughed. "Well, perhaps I sold the *same* information to more than one interested party."

"Information that undermines us, weakens us."

Taylor spread his hands, "Nothing Marstead can't recover from, I assure you."

He took a step toward her, still smiling. "Come on, Maggie. Let's not do this. Permit me to go my way—for old time's sake, eh? I have enough money saved to disappear; I won't be a bother to Marstead in the future."

"No. *Stay back*, Tay. My team will be here momentarily, but I will shoot you if I need to—and you know I *can* shoot."

Please. I don't want to shoot you, Taylor.

"Ah, dearest Mags, could you? Could you shoot me? *Me?* You have no idea how many times during training I fantasized about us, about holding your shimmering blonde hair between my fingers, about your long legs and you and me togeth—"

"Shut your filthy, lying mouth."

A car roared onto the bridge, then slowed. She spared it a fleeting glance; its passengers were not from Marstead, only curious onlookers who, upon seeing her gun, roared away as quickly as they'd arrived.

Taylor had timed his move to match Linnéa's momentary distraction. He was a tall man whose length spanned the distance between them. He lunged for her, swept her gun hand aside while squeezing, twisting her fingers and wrist.

The Beretta fired once before it dropped from Linnéa's numb, nerveless fingers without her say-so. The gun clattered onto the bridge, through the railing, and down, down, *down* to the dark, swirling water below.

Linnéa smacked Taylor's ear with a cupped palm and drove her knee into his groin. The instant he let go and fell back, she rammed her elbow up, clipping his jaw. He cursed but bulled forward, shoving her onto the bridge's ornate railing.

With his weight pressing her against the top rail, Linnéa's back was close to breaking. She was pinned, bowed backward, flailing, when he wrapped both hands about her throat. She attempted to jam her flattened hands between his arms to lever them apart, but he bent his elbows, pulled them together, and tucked them close to his chest—leaving no point of entry for her stiffened fingers. He pushed her harder until she was hanging out over the water, her feet dangling and thrashing above the bridge's walkway, while he tightened his grip on her throat, choking her.

She ripped and tore at his face; he laughed through clenched teeth. His eyes were . . . mad. Merciless. Insane.

She knew better than to scrabble at her attacker's hands, how futile and wasted any efforts to pry his fingers from her throat were, but the urge, *the need*, to free herself was desperate.

She had mere moments of consciousness left. While Weiß shouted from somewhere beyond the gray edges of her vision, she scratched and scored Taylor's hands with one hand. With the other, her injured hand, she reached into her upswept hair and yanked it loose.

The night before leaving Sweden, Laynie had spent an hour stropping the hair stick into a backup weapon. She'd honed the stick into a fine, razor-sharp shiv that glittered in the moonlight between her fingers. Taylor's maniacal gaze shifted to it too late. Linnéa drove the sharpened stiletto into the hollow between his collarbone and neck.

Shrieks split the night air as Taylor pulled away; Linnéa, teetering upon the railing, somehow managed to fall forward. She stumbled and crashed to her hands and knees, gasping, choking, coughing, then vomiting on the bridge's frozen sidewalk.

She raised her head, looking for Taylor, preparing to rise and defend herself again.

Her eyes encountered Weiß first. The errant shot from the Beretta had found him; he was kneeling in the street, groaning, holding his side.

She wrenched her eyes away from Weiß, seeking Taylor.

Finding him.

He leaned against his car's hood, staring at her. He had both hands pressed to his neck, but the blood pumping from his wound would not be staunched. Bloody foam burbled on his lips, while crimson rivulets spurted from between his fingers, ran down his arms and onto the hood, then dripped and drizzled upon the road.

As two cars raced onto the bridge and disgorged Marstead operatives, Taylor—his glazed eyes fixed on Linnéa—slid slowly down the hood to the car's grill and bumper and to the pavement. He sat upright for a moment, then tumbled over, his hands losing their hold on his neck.

Blood seeped from beneath him and pooled. Taylor still stared at Linnéa, but his eyes had lost their focus. He was gone.

Hands reached for her, lifted her up. "Are you all right?"

Linnéa shook them off. "No thanks to you! Where were you? *Why were you late?*"

"We . . . lost the cab in the fog." The shamefaced agent, a stranger, held out her pocketbook. "This is yours, I believe? You must be freezing. Come on, get in the car."

She spat at him—at all of them. "Take care of them, but leave me alone!"

Staggering a step back, she found her shoes and slipped them on, collected her stole, dragged it over her shoulders, and watched. They were "cleaning" the scene with urgent haste, getting done what they could before the police arrived.

Two operatives shoved Weiß into the back seat of one car; others piled Taylor's body into his car's trunk and drove the vehicle away.

Soon all that remained of those harrowing minutes on the bridge were Linnéa, a single Marstead auto, two operatives, and Taylor's life-blood congealing on the icy pavement.

"Let's go!" the same agent insisted, touching Laynie's elbow.

She jerked away. She was too angry to go with them. Too filled with sorrow.

"Give me a minute," she whispered. "Go on ahead. I need . . . I need to walk."

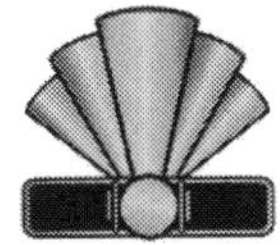

POSTSCRIPT

LINNÉA ADJUSTED HER bedraggled stole and made for the other side of the bridge. One stocking was torn, her steps in the high heels wobbled, and her body shook—chilled not by the cold but by Taylor's betrayal and the terror she'd endured, a terror she had beaten only by taking his life . . . the life of another human being.

"But I'm alive," she whispered. "I'm alive because I killed him. I had no other choice."

Behind her, she heard the first, faint warbles of police sirens. She would have to get off the bridge and move away from it or risk being picked up for questioning—and that would not do. She had bruises on the tender skin of her neck and Taylor's blood on her hands and dress, blood that matched the frozen puddles at the center of the bridge.

She picked up her pace, anger and shock beginning to bleed off, replaced by what was necessary and expedient.

She had rounded the far base of the bridge so that she was walking parallel to the river when something stirred down deep within her. Whatever it was, it uncurled and settled there. Linnéa stopped, stared out at the water, and dared to touch that "thing" in her soul, to know it and put a name to it.

It was a conviction, cold and solid. It was an unalterable decision.

She would remain with Marstead and serve as they asked her—she would continue on, push and claw her way forward, exceed her handlers' and superiors' expectations, defeat trepidation and self-doubt, and *win* at this "game" of espionage.

"Whatever the cost," she whispered.

I have killed now.

To go forward, I must overcome narrowmindedness, set aside the squeamish morals of my youth—those things that bind me, that make me ineffective, a danger to my craft.

She would embrace and, without qualms or further guilt, use the power her body gave her over men, even strong, powerful men . . . *and their secrets.*

The love she had felt for Black?

Extinguished.

Dead.

She would never offer it to another.

I must harden myself, become whatever and whomever I must become . . . to steal what I must steal.

Linnéa nodded to herself, acknowledging her resolve. She walked on, calm and steady.

Wiser in the ways of the world.

Mama, Dad, and Sammie must never know what I really do, what I have become. They cannot know what I've traded for the greater good.

"'*For the greater good*'?" another Voice whispered.

Such a tender, gentle Voice it was! So gentle, that its next words did not immediately bite or sting.

"*Have you convinced yourself that sin can be 'good,' under some circumstances? Or are you employing 'the greater good' as justification for your sins—so that you will feel righteous in your own eyes? So you might avoid admitting how lost you are?*

Come to me, child. I will find you and take you home."

Home.

The whispered caress flew Linnéa Olander from Hamburg across oceans and continents; it conveyed her back in time, two decades and more. Three-year-old Laynie Portland nestled in her mama's sweet, chocolate-hued embrace. Polly's comforting arms held her close and rocked her back and forth. Little Laynie snuggled against Polly's bosom. She even felt the drowsy tug of sleep as her mama sang to her.

"*Yes, Jesus loves me,*" Mama crooned in Laynie's ear. "*Yes, Jesus loves me.*"

Mama's warm breath kissed her forehead. "*Do you know how much Jesus loves you, sugar? He loves you so much that he will wash you clean, give you a new heart, take away all your shame, and never, ever leave you.*"

Linnéa hummed the chorus; her memories filled in the lyrics, "Yes, Jesus loves me, yes, Jesus loves me."

Does Jesus love me? Is that true? Did he ever love me?

No. I have never been worthy of his love.

She shuddered and shook herself, continued walking until she reached the next corner. Ahead and to the right a car drew to the curb. She recognized the agent in the passenger seat attempting to make eye contact with her.

Marstead. They'd arrived too late to save her; now they wanted to whisk her away.

"*Jesus will never leave you, Laynie, sugar. He done made that a promise.*"

"I don't think that promise applies to me, Mama."

Linnéa moved her hand an inch or two, a twitch only, signaling the agent that she'd seen him. The car eased down the street and turned left to a less conspicuous pickup location. A minute later, Linnéa crossed the street and turned left, too.

As she reached for the car's door handle, her mother's voice, denying the frigid night, warmed her cheeks like a waft of balmy air.

It breathed into her heart, "*Do you know how much Jesus loves you, sugar?*"

No Mama, it's far too late for me—and perhaps it always has been. I'm set on this course. There's no turning back now.

She slid into the rear seat.

"Drive," she ordered.

THE END

Read on for a preview of
Laynie Portland, Retired Spy.

My Dear Readers,

I HOPE YOU ENJOYED this introduction to the **Laynie Portland** series. Page ahead to explore the beginnings of the next book in the series, *Laynie Portland, Retired Spy*. This full-length novel is filled with more twists and turns than the tallest, fastest roller coaster in North America, Six Flags' *Kingda Ka*, and its epic *Zumanjaro: Drop of Doom*. (*Grin* Yes, I love roller coasters!)

As you begin the next leg of your journey with Laynie in *Retired Spy* (and if you are new to my writing), you may also begin to realize that Laynie's "backstory" is not complete. If you are interested in the very first glimpse of Laynie in my books, check out my series, **A Prairie Heritage**. This eight-book series follows the same family across many generations. Laynie does not make her entrance until Book 7; however, as my guests, I invite you to enjoy the first three full-length books in the series **without cost** by downloading the eBook, ***A Prairie Heritage: The Early Years***, from your preferred eBook retailer.

Thank you. I appreciate your readership and the fellowship we share in Jesus.

—*Vikki*

Author's Note

THE SOVIET UNION officially dissolved on December 26, 1991. Its former Soviet republics became independent nations; Russia emerged as the Russian Federation.

In 1995, as is forecast in the Prologue of *Laynie Portland, Retired Spy*, the FSK, Russia's Federal Counterintelligence Service and heir to the KGB, became the Federal Security Service of the Russian Federation, the FSB, by order of President Boris Yeltsin.

Laynie Portland
RETIRED SPY

A PREVIEW

LP

PROLOGUE

STOCKHOLM, SWEDEN, AUGUST 1994

"YOU WANT TO TAKE A LEAVE of absence? What, *now?* No. *Nej.* Absolutely not."

"I put in for the time weeks ago, sir; I was told my request was approved."

"Well, this letter changes everything: Petroff is the payoff for your years of work, Linnéa: He's not just a 'big fish'; he's the catch of the century. We lost our last opportunity to hook him—as I shouldn't have to remind you. I can't allow you to screw it up a second time."

Lars Alvarsson studied the woman standing before his desk: She was tall and slim but shapely in all the right places, even for a woman on the far end of her thirties. Milky-soft blue eyes appraised him from beneath a graceful upsweep of dark blonde hair.

She projected intelligence. Composure. Confidence.

But it was the rare glimpse—only a hint—of vulnerability that set her apart in a room of beautiful women; it was the allure that drew intelligent and powerful men to her.

Alvarsson had never been able to decide if the intimation of fragility was her natural personality surfacing or if it was yet another facet of her skills—for this woman was, by far, the best actor he'd worked with in his professional capacity.

Dressed in tasteful simplicity, she could have posed for a photo layout captioned, "Today's Consummate Female Swedish Professional"—except that she was not Swedish. Outside the tight circle of her Marstead supervisors, *no one* acquainted with this woman knew that she was born an American, recruited straight out of the University of Washington in her early twenties, transplanted to Sweden, and "attached" to a family that had lived for generations in a village not far from Uppsala.

Her real name was not Linnéa Olander.

It was Helena Portland—Helena, pronounced heh-*LAY*-nuh—although she had always insisted that she be called "Laynie."

Laynie Portland.

The woman lifted her chin and met Alvarsson's gaze. "I would not ask, but it is important. A family matter, sir."

My only sister is getting married in two weeks. In a rural, backwater, American farming community, of all places. I need to be with her on her wedding day.

I promised.

She did not speak those words aloud. She had kept her boss and his superiors ignorant of her sister's existence. Alvarsson knew of Laynie's adoptive parents in Seattle. He knew that her only brother and his wife had died in a car crash eight months ago, orphaning their two little ones. And, as far as he knew or cared, the children's maternal grandparents had assumed guardianship of the children.

He did not know about Kari or that the children, Shannon and Robbie, were with her now.

Kari, my sister. You searched for me; you hunted high and low, and you found me—after a lifetime apart!

No, Laynie had taken pains to ensure that her watchful, jealous employers did not know about her sister.

Kari was safer that way.

The scowl Alvarsson turned on her was as unsympathetic as it was unyielding. "You don't have a family, Linnéa, remember? With the exception of a single, covert holiday in the U.S. once a year, you gave them up. That was the deal, and it hasn't changed."

"Sir—"

"*No.* Regardless of how careful we are, returning you to the States hazards blowing your cover and exposing the Company. And the risks don't even speak to the expense. To transition you from Stockholm to the U.S. in your previous identity requires the allocation and coordination of many resources, and each operation sets Marstead back something in the realm of a hundred thousand dollars."

Marstead International: "the Company." A respected and flourishing enterprise with a global reach but, unknown to a large slice of its employees, Marstead was also a well-developed front for a joint American and NATO Alliance intelligence agency with its largest office located in Stockholm, Sweden—even though Sweden was *not* a member of NATO, that nation preferring a neutral position in the world's conflicts. On Marstead's part, basing many of its operations out of Stockholm had been intentional, a means of functioning in plain sight and close proximity to the Soviet Union (today the Russian Federation).

"We permitted you to take emergency leave to attend your brother's funeral back in January; that was your vacation for the year. You aren't owed more leave at this time—we're still paying the price of your last one! During that unscheduled, three-week absence, Petroff's ardor cooled, and we lost our window, our opportunity to intercept the Russians' new laser schematics."

"I am aware, sir."

As if I weren't conscious of the setback; it has taken six months of tedious, cautious maneuvering to reignite Petroff's interest.

Alvarsson raised one eyebrow. "Are you, Linnéa? Do you grasp the long-term implications? If you do, if you care so much about those people in the States you call 'family'—and if you are concerned at all for your own skin—then you know exactly *why* we cannot have you jaunting off to the States at this crucial juncture."

Alvarsson steepled his hands in a judicious manner. "Hear me on this, Olander: Our sources tell us that your Russian 'friend' already has his people doing a deep dive into your background. Right now—at this very moment—his people are scouring your family tree, your education, your work history, your travel records. We cannot afford to take any chances."

He added, almost as an afterthought, "You don't become the exclusive plaything of a formidable, highly placed Russian politician without coming under great scrutiny first."

Exclusive plaything.

Inwardly, Linnéa flinched, but she never flicked an eye or moved a muscle. She understood her role. It was the daily bread of her work—guiding the selected "man of the hour" through the phases of infatuation, romance, affection, love, and trust. Followed by betrayal.

Linnéa had accrued her sordid skills through the Company's rigorous tradecraft training program. She had learned well; she was good, *very* good, at her job.

My life may have no value, but the information I gather does.

With the dissolution of the Soviet Union in 1991, the Cold War had come to an end. In the Russian political and economic upheaval that followed, the city of St. Petersburg—Russia's gateway to the Baltic Sea—became a thriving hub of Russian scientific discovery and technological innovation. St. Petersburg was rich in culture, and it was burgeoning with opportunity.

St. Petersburg was Linnéa's hunting ground.

Marstead operated a branch office in St. Petersburg, and Linnéa traveled from Stockholm to St. Petersburg each month, ostensibly to work her Russian Marstead accounts. In reality, she spent her evenings trolling the night clubs and hot spots where bored, overworked scientists, engineers, and inventors came to refresh themselves.

She was cautious, and she chose her marks herself—until Petroff arrived. Vassili Aleksandrovich Petroff, brilliant scientist, wealthy Russian powerbroker and politician, lived in Moscow and normally worked there. He breathed the rarified air of the Russian Federation's Security Council on a daily basis, serving as Secretary Rushailo's personal technology advisor.

With Petroff's appearance, Marstead's interests shifted. Petroff was a man whose access to state secrets could satisfy Marstead's intelligence needs for years. He possessed every quality Marstead desired, rolled into a single mark, but he was a man beyond Marstead's reach until, just over a year ago, Petroff's official duties required his occasional, *ad hoc* presence in St Petersburg.

According to Marstead's ubiquitous intelligence sources, Petroff was seeking a suitable long-term companion—a woman of the world; his equal, intellectually and socially; a suitable trophy to flaunt before his friends, but also a beauty who would be suited to Petroff's public life.

Approaching his mid-forties, he was tall and lean and still owned a full head of sandy-colored hair. From a distance he projected a mild, naturally curious, perhaps bookish countenance, particularly when he swept aside the front locks of his hair with unconscious indifference.

Linnéa's superiors pulled her off her other assignments and ordered her to focus her attentions on Petroff. Under Marstead's orders, Linnéa studied Petroff; she "learned" the man. She was to win her way into a long-term relationship with the man. If Linnéa conducted herself well, if she ingratiated herself into the Russian's life, Petroff was to be her next (and possibly her last) mark.

And so, for the past year, Linnéa had refrained from seducing new targets, and Marstead had scheduled Linnéa's visits to St. Petersburg and her sorties into the city's club life to correspond with the dates of Petroff's visits. With careful deliberation, Linnéa had edged her way nearer to Petroff's orbit.

She'd had brief encounters with him in the past year, moments that amounted to little more than cordial familiarity. But—finally—on her last trip to St. Petersburg, she'd arranged herself so that Petroff "stumbled" upon her, and they had spent several uninterrupted hours talking over drinks in a quiet side room of a luxury club. She had kept her part of the conversation witty and cerebral, making him laugh and relax. She'd spoken openly of her position with Marstead and had expounded with expertise and insight on the current technology market.

She had learned that Petroff was a man who sought to own the best of everything; thus, Linnéa had demonstrated that she was far more than arm candy or an inconsequential one-night stand. She believed she'd left Petroff that evening with the impression that Linnéa Olander could be a complement to both his brains and his *savoir-faire*: a beautiful, accomplished, and independent woman. A rare commodity. *A match.*

Linnéa had declined his invitation that evening to a nightcap in his hotel room. She would string him along until they were further acquainted. It was essential that she prove worthy of his enduring attentions.

She had, she believed, left him wanting more.

Nevertheless, as Alvarsson intimated, it was important to fully prepare herself for what could lie ahead, because the risk of entering into a long-term relationship with him had more than one dangerous facet.

First, the man was fascinating. Brilliant. Not to be underestimated. *Ever*. In his younger years, Petroff's unsuspecting adversaries had ascribed a boyish naiveté to him. Many had found that assumption to be a costly, even a deadly, mistake. Up close, his gentle, probing brown eyes had revealed a shrewd and calculating mind.

Second, Petroff was possessive. Nothing he considered "his" was permitted outside his watchful control. If Linnéa succeeded in attaching herself to Petroff, the 'relationship' would likely become restrictive. Even oppressive.

Third, Linnéa worried that her meticulous backstory might not stand up under *this* man's scrutiny, because Petroff was more than political: He was a former agent of the now-defunct KGB—and once KGB, *always* KGB. Sure, the KGB had been replaced by the FSK, the Federal Counterintelligence Service (even though Linnéa had heard whispers that the FSK itself might soon be going through yet another makeover and name change under the Russian Federation's President, Boris Yeltsin). Regardless of its name, the FSK had inherited many of its players from the ranks of the former KGB. This meant Petroff was both connected and influential.

Dangerous.

Petroff has remained friends with his former KGB comrades, those who still have authority and influence. They provide him the means to sniff out and dissect my background, perhaps uncover my former life. My family.

She shuddered to consider what Petroff might do to her parents or her sister's family should he come to trust Linnéa and discover that his trust had been betrayed.

It was under the shadow of such jeopardy that "Linnéa Olander" lived in deep cover. For that reason, every part of Linnéa's Marstead cover was strictly controlled. Nothing—not love, not family, not choice—was allowed to compromise the sanctity of her Swedish identity.

When it came to her family, Linnéa was grateful for Marstead's stringent security constraints.

The final danger Petroff presented had dawned as an unsettling revelation to Laynie: Petroff held an attraction for her that was . . . *troubling*. What Linnéa saw of Petroff somehow moved her, spoke to her in strange ways, and his boyish good looks and energy never ceased to raise her heartrate.

Why? Why this man? Why do I feel such attraction for him? Such untapped emotion when I'm with him?

As jaded as her heart had grown through her various love affairs, it was a new and disturbing experience for Laynie to find herself pulled toward a mark. She might be tempted to give more than her body to this dangerous man—even after she had heard the tales circulating about him . . .

PETROFF WAS KNOWN as a connoisseur of fine things—he employed the best tailors, drove the best cars, drank the finest wines and vodka, ate the choicest foods—and only sparingly, for he despised overindulgence. He was also a lover of art, music, architecture, and . . . dogs. His favored breed was the *Chornyi Terrier*, known in the west as the Black Russian Terrier.

The breed was developed in the Soviet Union during the late 1940s and the early 1950s for use as military dogs. The breed's pedigree included lines from the Giant Schnauzer, Airedale Terrier, Rottweiler, and other guard and working dogs. In show, the *Chornyi* closely resembled the Giant Schnauzer; in comportment, the dog was protective and fearless, often thought by its owners (to their amazement) to be more intelligent than they were.

As Petroff made the rounds of the St. Petersburg clubs, a disturbing story circulated with him, a tale of Petroff's favorite *Chornyi*, Alina, a female dog he had hand-raised from a pup. Petroff doted on her. Alina traveled everywhere with Petroff, slept in his room at night, and served as a further layer of personal protection after his bodyguards.

According to the rumors swirling in Petroff's wake, on a certain trip, unexpected celebratory fireworks had so disturbed Alina that she had become terrified and had run off, ignoring Petroff's repeated commands to come to him. When Petroff's people located the dog two days later and brought her back, Petroff had pulled his sidearm and shot the dog in the head.

He had said in the hearing of his people (so the anecdote went), "I will not tolerate the disobedience of something I own. There can be no forgiveness for disloyalty."

According to the rumors, Petroff treated his women with similar possessiveness. As long as a woman held his attention, he kept a jealous leash on her—although most endured only a night or, if particularly engaging, a week or a month. When he was finished with a woman, when he no longer found her of interest, he cast her aside.

But there were also stories of Petroff's longer-term women, of which only two were known. One, it was said, displeased Petroff's sense of ownership: He had beaten her senseless. The other, a Lebanese beauty, turned out not to be Lebanese, but Israeli. A spy.

The woman traveled with Petroff when he left to visit Islamabad on state business. When he returned to Moscow, she did not.

Linnéa shuddered a second time. *I am to be the bait on the end of this hook; I must be careful, so much more careful than I have ever needed to be.*

Still, the thought of being with Petroff aroused feelings in her, feelings that surprised and concerned her. *Why am I like this?* she asked herself. *Why am I so cold and unfeeling toward a decent man but drawn to someone who would snap my neck should the circumstance dictate?*

A familiar voice in her head sneered, *Because you don't deserve a "good" man, Laynie.*

"MISS OLANDER! Are you listening?"

"Of course, sir."

Considering the subject closed, Alvarsson focused on his calendar. Today's date nudged them closer to the end of August, and the northern hemisphere was still in the grip of summer. "If you play your cards right, Linnéa, Petroff will have you installed in his Moscow apartment by Christmas."

He fixed her with another glare. "This assignment is too important to jeopardize for any reason. It is *your job*, this once-in-a-lifetime opportunity, to convince Petroff that *you* are the woman he's been looking for—not for another tryst or fling, but for a long-term relationship."

Linnéa inclined her head. "Of course, sir. Petroff wants someone with whom he can share his life, a companion who is his intellectual equal and who shares his passion for technology. A woman who can be an asset to him in his social circle. An acquisition he can flaunt—not merely an escort or a temporary lover. To that end, I must cultivate the cerebral and companionship aspects of our relationship. I will, initially, resist intimate overtures. I mustn't yield to him too quickly; the 'courtship' and pursuit must prove my worth to him."

Linnéa said nothing further as the tenderly nurtured prospect of seeing her sister again died.

Alvarsson was right. She had a job to do, a crucial role to play. Nothing took precedence over the job; everything gave way to it. The job was all that mattered.

The job was espionage.

Linnéa was a spy, and her *modus operandi* was seduction.

Her work was "appropriating" emerging technology and other classified information from America's strongest rival.

This week, after painstaking months of careful moves, her relationship with Petroff had taken a desired turn: He had sent Linnéa a short letter—an invitation—via her Stockholm office.

Others read Linnéa's mail before she did, another aspect of Marstead's supervision of Linnéa's cover. They would read and approve her reply, too, before it was sent.

"How do you propose to respond to Petroff's invitation?" Alvarsson asked.

He held the single sheet between two fingers, re-reading it.

Linnéa had scanned it once and memorized it.

My dear Miss Olander,

I find myself thinking on our last conversation in St. Petersburg, and I would enjoy the opportunity to continue it. The seaside in late summer holds many pleasures, and I have time to indulge in a holiday. I own a modest *dacha* on the shore of the Caspian, and my yacht is moored nearby. The sea is open to us for adventure, be it swimming, snorkeling, fishing, or bathing in the sun.

If you were able to arrange your busy schedule so as to spend a week with me, I would send my private jet to fly you from Stockholm to Grozny on August 26. I would personally meet you in Grozny and escort you to my *dacha*.

Miss Olander, if you accept my invitation, I promise to pamper you during the day, while we explore the delights of evening together. Whatever you wish will be my command: exquisite food and fine wines, music, dancing—and, perhaps, more. I hope to receive your reply soon.

With great admiration,
Vassili Aleksandrovich

The letter's tone was confident—as though, by crooking his finger, she would do his bidding—and he had signed the correspondence with his first and patronymic names, a familiarity. But the coveted invitation, arriving so close to Kari's wedding in early September, couldn't have come at a worse time.

"Miss Olander." Alvarsson was staring at her.

"Yes, sir?"

"How do you propose to respond to Petroff's invitation? August 26 is next Friday."

Linnéa cleared her throat. "I will accept his invitation with an apologetic limitation: I will only be able to stay the weekend—three nights. Work obligations require that I return to Stockholm Monday morning, August 29."

Alvarsson nodded his approval. "A good strategy. Two days and three nights. Time enough to deepen the acquaintance but stave off sleeping with him. A taste of your companionship to leave him wanting more."

"Yes."

"Write your response to him, then go shopping; you'll need a new wardrobe."

"Yes, sir."

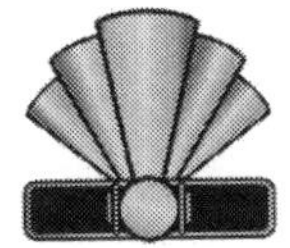

Chapter 1

LP

Summer, 2001
Lake Komsomolskoye, Northeastern Russia

LINNÉA WRESTLED THE Gucci bag from the top of the bedroom closet. She opened it on the bed and began to pack. Her maid, Alyona, hovered nearby.

"Mistress, what are you doing? May I be of help?"

Linnéa knew that Alyona's question, "What are you doing?" not her, "May I be of help?" was uppermost in the maid's concern. Linnéa never went anywhere, not out of the *dacha*, not into another room, not even to the toilet without Alyona's ubiquitous, hovering presence nearby. And should Linnéa do anything unplanned or out of the ordinary—such as an unscheduled, unsanctioned walk along the lakeshore before breakfast?—Alyona was charged with knowing (and reporting) Linnéa's unexpected activity posthaste.

Whatever attraction or "pull" toward Petroff Linnéa had experienced in the early days of their relationship had withered and died under his controlling hand. Linnéa had struggled, had labored under the constraints, had wrestled against depression and despair, but she had *not* withered; she had not died within.

Not as yet . . . although she teetered on the edge.

"Since Vassili Aleksandrovich has been called back to Moscow, I have decided to drive into St. Petersburg this morning," Linnéa replied without looking up. "I will be gone two nights only, at the most three, to check in at my office. My quarterly report is a month past due. I also wish to do a little shopping, perhaps spend a day at a spa."

Alyona's fingers twined together; it was a nervous habit. "You gave me no notice, Mistress, or I would have packed your bag and been prepared to travel with you."

"I hardly require your services for such a short trip; when I have finished my business, I will return to our house outside Moscow. I wish you, in the meantime, to attend to our apartment in the city this afternoon. Ready it for Vassili Aleksandrovich, should he wish to sleep there this evening."

"But . . ." Alyona fidgeted further. "This is highly irregular, Mistress. Is . . . does Master Petroff know your plans?"

For seven years, Linnéa had played Petroff's game, and for seven years, she had played her own game, right beneath his nose. It had taken all her skills of subterfuge, her strength of will, and her loyalty to the Company, but she had succeeded beyond Marstead's wildest dreams.

If Petroff's superiors were to ever learn the volume and importance of the intel the mistress to the Russian technology czar had "acquired," and if the Security Council were to discover how she had, subsequently, conveyed that intel to a joint NATO intelligence alliance? The revelations would rock the Russian government to its core and would earn Petroff a slow, painful death in the dank basement torture and execution chambers of Lubyanka Prison.

Yes, the rewards were well worth the risk, but the "game" had cost Linnéa. The price had been years of her freedom—a price she was no longer able to pay.

She was exhausted. Worn. Frayed.

Like finely spun silk stretched beyond its capacity, the network of threads holding her façade of composure together might rend and give way without warning, leaving in its place a gaping hole. The walls in her psyche separating farce from reality, madness from sanity, possessed the strength and resiliency of wet tissue paper.

I've had enough.

I want out.

I need *out.*

Linnéa had sublimated so much of her will and identity to Petroff's control that she recently found herself wondering, *Who am I?* and, *Why am I?* And while those questions of being and purpose resounded in her head with growing intensity, another force bubbled within her. More powerful than responsibility or logic, it was the acute awareness of a growing emotion, a primal sensation that terrified her because she had so little control over it.

Rage.

Rage burned in her with a fervor that defied duty and obligation, that required every ounce of Linnéa's training to stem—because she no longer had the desire to restrain or suppress it. Suppress it? *No.* Linnéa yearned to release the rage; she wanted it to burst from her mouth and from her hands. She imagined acts of violence against those who, at Petroff's command, kept her on a leash . . . and she daydreamed of setting Petroff's bed on fire—with him in it.

How long can I continue to do this? How much more can I endure before I shatter and give myself away?

"Mistress?" Alyona repeated.

Linnéa's Marstead sources had sussed out Alyona's background: Petroff had handpicked the maid—a Belarusian close in age to Linnéa—from the ranks of the Red Army. Linnéa did not need Marstead's sources to tell her that Alyona was Petroff's first line of supervision and control over Linnéa. The woman had been Linnéa's "maid" and keeper for the past three years.

During that time, Linnéa had hidden her real emotions from the woman, but it was getting harder as time wore on . . . and as the day of her deliverance drew near.

This morning, Alyona's impertinence came perilously close to igniting the rebellion Linnéa had envisioned too often of late. She unbent and fixed the woman with a cold stare. "Are you questioning me, Alyona? Perhaps I should slap the presumption from your mouth."

Oh . . . how good that felt!

Linnéa had never before threatened Alyona. The woman's expression froze, and her usually florid complexion drained to a mottled white.

"I-I beg your pardon, Mistress. I will . . . I will leave you now to-to arrange the car and driver for you."

"You do that," Linnéa whispered to the maid's back.

Careful! Oh, please be careful! the voice of sanity and self-preservation urged her, but she cared less at this point than she had in years past.

She calmed and resumed her packing, readying herself for the coming confrontation. But moments after the maid conjured an excuse to leave the room, Linnéa anticipated that the man to whom she was companion and mistress would storm into the bedroom of their lavish cottage to confront her.

Linnéa, get a grip! You cannot allow yourself the luxury of letting your anger bleed through; you must not rouse his suspicions.

She was expecting his furious roar and did not flinch when he threw open the bedroom door, sending it crashing against the wall, rattling the cottage's windowpanes.

"What is this? Where the **blank** do you think you are going?"

With a placid mien firmly in place—the one she had perfected during her years with Petroff—Linnéa glanced up from her packing.

"Ah, my love. There you are!" She tucked her makeup bag and a small box of jewelry into the suitcase before she turned to him.

"Your being called back to Moscow today provides the perfect opportunity for me to hand in my quarterly report. As I told you last week and reminded you yesterday, I am overdue at my office."

She chuckled softly. "Despite how I enjoy the lake and the forest, I cannot be on holiday forever, you know."

"I told you to *quit that job*, Linnéa! For the past five years I have ordered you to quit—and still you defy me!"

He towered over her, crowding her personal space. Glowering. Shaking with rage, fists clenching and unclenching.

Linnéa did not shrink; she straightened and faced him. She was a tall woman herself, but her uplifted chin scarcely reached his shoulders. She placed her hands upon his chest and smiled her best smile—the one that dimpled both sides of her mouth in innocent, girlish fashion. She knew what was needed and looked past his fury, deep into his eyes, disclosing her soul to him. Offering him deference. Making herself submissive. Acquiescent. Adoring.

"You know my heart belongs to you, мой любимый, *moy lyubimyy*—my love. My job is but a distraction for those times when we cannot be together. Please do not deny me this little thing, this trifling diversion."

"Deny? You speak of *deny?* I have denied you nothing, Linnéa. I have given you everything a woman could wish for—a grand house outside of Moscow, an extravagant apartment in the city, this lakeside *dacha*, another cottage by the sea, a yacht, and money to shop the finest stores in the world. So! So, what have I ever denied you? Eh?"

Only my freedom, Linnéa thought. *But after all these years in service to my country, I shall soon take back my life.*

Linnéa leaned into his chest, lifting her chin higher, baring her neck and making herself vulnerable to him. She never pled or wheedled—Petroff despised whining in any form. Rather, she "capitulated" her desires, providing him the opportunity to bestow his munificence upon her.

As a benevolent tyrant.

A tyrant, nonetheless.

"Why, Vassili Aleksandrovich, you yourself told me last evening that you must leave for Moscow this morning, *nyet?* And after you have gone, what is here for me? The days . . . and the nights will be unbearable. And you will be busy for long hours in Moscow—unable even to come home and sleep with me, will you not? This checking in with my company will amuse and divert me a little from your absence.

"So, then: I shall complete this business, shop a bit, perhaps pamper myself at a spa, and then come home to await your return."

He searched her face, searching it for deceit and finding nothing but what Linnéa wanted him to see. Then he could not help himself. His arms came up and wrapped themselves around her; he pressed her close to his chest—not in selfless affection, but in the pride and power of ownership—for whatever Petroff "loved," he had a pathological need to possess completely. Linnéa was a beautiful, intelligent, and successful woman, a jewel Petroff owned body and soul, a pearl he flaunted before the world as his and his alone.

"It is true that I have been summoned to a special assembly of the Security Council. Some emergency of state over rumors of an impending attack on high-value targets of unknown number, the information coming to us via a source I have little confidence in. However, Secretary Rushailo *himself* wishes me on hand for my technological advice, should he require it."

As with many powerful men who felt their vaunted positions were unassailable, Petroff's pride was his weakness. He trusted his patrons and inner circle and believed the rules of operational security applied only to those peons below him. In his efforts to augment his self-importance, he was frequently not as circumspect as his position warranted.

Linnéa's unspoken opinion was that Russian politicians on the Security Council and their advisors lived in a state of perpetual agitation, reminding her of the characters in a folk story who cried over and over, "The sky is falling! The sky is falling!" Nevertheless, she assiduously gathered and passed on to her superiors the crumbs Petroff's carelessness let drop.

Feigning concern, Linnéa's brow furrowed. "An attack? Will you be safe, my love?"

"*Da*, without a doubt. I surmised from the call that it was not a threat toward the Motherland, and I am not certain how much credence I give the intelligence—coming through Afghani sources—but I cannot decline the summons. However, if the situation clears quickly, I will return here, perhaps as early as tomorrow evening."

Still chewing on where the supposed attack might be aimed and hoping to pass the nugget on to her superiors without delay, Linnéa pouted. "Ah, my darling! We both know our holiday is over, do we not? For the sake of the Council's safety, they will keep you in seclusion for a week, perhaps two. I might just as well return to Moscow and wait for your return to our house or apartment—equally alone in either place—*or* . . . or I can take advantage of the present crisis to visit my office in St. Petersburg so that, afterward, my time is all yours as it should be. I hope you will not say no, Vassi."

Linnéa willed her eyes to moisten just a little and blinked to push the gleam of unshed tears to the corners of her eyes. "This job helps me bear the lonely hours until we are together again."

Petroff's grip loosened marginally. "Marstead knows how vital my connections and favor are to their success in Russia. They are aware that I wish you near me at all times; for this, they should make allowances."

"Just so! But your superiors will keep you sequestered until the present crisis passes, and while they keep you, I cannot be with you, can I? It is only two nights in St. Petersburg, Vassi, *zvezdochka*—my star—two nights I would be alone in our bed, without you, missing you.

"Save me from such longing, Vassili Aleksandrovich! I shall drive into the city this morning and check in with Marstead, *pro forma*. Nyström will give me my next assignment, and I shall return to you with another list of upcoming technological exhibits you and I will enjoy visiting and scientific breakthroughs on which I am to write my reports. This I do for them every quarter, as you know—although my present report is quite past due."

He pursed his lips and regarded her, hovering between admiration and puzzlement, even as his anger slipped a little. "Truly, I do not understand you sometimes, Linnéa. You do not need this 'job' as you call it."

"Need? No, I need for nothing, Vassili Aleksandrovich, nothing except *you*. You have made me your queen, and you shower me with luxury and your love." Linnéa dimpled again. "You even allow me my insignificant pet projects."

The former KGB officer studied her, finding nothing duplicitous in her words or expression. Only adulation. He sighed. "I wish you always near me, Linnéa."

"*Dal''she ot glaz—blizhe k serdtsu.* Further from the eye—closer to the heart, my darling. These infrequent trips to my office in St. Petersburg and my little assignments away from you? They keep our loving fresh . . . and thrilling, do they not?"

She winked and whispered the promise of something racy she would buy in St. Petersburg and model for him when they were reunited in Moscow.

He grinned, then roared a laugh in response.

Linnéa grinned back, even as she wondered how much longer such wiles would work on him. So much of her "free" time was given over to the beauty treatments and rigorous workout schedule that kept her body as lithe, youthful, and attractive as possible despite the inexorable advance of age.

Her looks and sweet compliance were the sole means by which she navigated the labyrinth of Petroff's shifting moods: cloying, spiteful control at one end of the spectrum and lavish overindulgence at the other.

With fits of cruelty and physical abuse sprinkled between.

He sobered and cleared his throat. "Are you all right, Linnéa? I did not hurt you last evening, did I? If only you would not anger me so . . ."

Linnéa's smile did not falter. "I am yours, Vassi. I did not mean to displease you. I am sorry."

She had iced the lump on her temple. Makeup would cover the bruise, but she could do nothing for the blood that had seeped into the sclera in the outside corner of her left eye. Would he refuse to let her appear in public because of it?

"What of this?" He caressed her temple with his thumb, indicating the blood-red stain in her eye.

She shrugged. "It is nothing. Everyone has, on occasion, scratched or poked themselves while sleeping and wakened to a reddened eye, is this not so?"

He grunted, over his "remorse." "*Da*, this is so. And you have this report of yours ready? It will project Russia's technological advances in a favorable light?"

"But of course." Linnéa smiled once more, knowing she had won. She gestured toward the portfolio atop her laptop, both lying on the bed next to her handbag. "Do you wish to review the report before I hand it in?"

He had already seen it—Linnéa knew Alyona had slipped him the portfolio, then returned it.

Because nothing I do goes unreported.

"No, but if you insist upon this trip, Alyona must accompany you," Petroff announced. "I will also send Zakhar with you. It is not right for the woman of such an important Russian man to traipse about the country without a proper escort."

"Alyona's assistance will be welcome, and Zakhar's help with the traffic and crowds of St. Petersburg will be appreciated."

Linnéa knew how to "negotiate" with Petroff to procure the best situation she could hope for. Although she had expected to be strapped with Alyona and a driver, she had harbored a very small hope that she might manage to leave without the company of Zakhar, the dour, middle-aged lout who, like Alyona, dogged Linnéa's every step.

Zakhar was ex-Soviet military and loyal only to Petroff—another element of Petroff's elaborate, layered ring of supervision and control over her.

Dimitri Ilyich Zakhar! She loathed Petroff's single-minded lapdog and the way how he stared at her, undressing her with his eyes, the red birthmark that ran from his throat up the right side of his cheek darkening with lust as he watched her.

Linnéa shuddered.

"And you will keep your mobile phone with you at all times so I may reach you?"

Only one response was acceptable.

"Certainly, Vassili."

The phone was the electronic leash that tethered her to him. She dared go nowhere without it—or ever turn it off. And woe be to her if she neglected to keep it charged!

Linnéa would check in with her St. Petersburg office later today, and she would find out if Alvarsson and his Marstead superiors had approved her request to quit the field and "come in from the cold." If so, Nyström, her St. Petersburg boss, would deploy resources to facilitate her escape from Zakhar and Alyona's overwatch, either this afternoon or, at the latest, tomorrow.

I am so close to freedom! I can—I must—keep it together a little longer.

Linnéa tried not to envision a scenario in which her Company superiors turned down her request. The possibilities crept in anyway.

What if they will not pull me out? If they insist that I stay?

But I cannot maintain this façade forever. I am forty-six years old now. True, Petroff does not keep me only for sex. No, and he has never been 'faithful' to me in that regard—it was not agreed to. But I know he is growing restless, dissatisfied with me. The beatings come more frequently, and he is less remorseful after.

How long before he perceives that I am aging, before he no longer desires me? How long until he finds a younger, more accomplished woman, and his admiration for me pales in comparison?

If he were to take a new mistress, would he simply allow me to return to Sweden? I cannot believe so: I am too well known in his circles; it would prick his pride to allow me my freedom.

If—**no, when**—*he drops me for another woman, he will not let me go—for he would not be able to tolerate the idea, even the remote possibility, that another man might have me. He could not abide that. I would, I think, simply disappear . . . as so many of his enemies have.*

She also played out a terrifying scenario in her thoughts where Petroff held her in tender embrace and whispered in her ear, "Do you think me so naïve, *kotyonok moya*, my kitten? I have known from the beginning who you were: a spy for the Americans and their NATO lackeys.

"I have enjoyed our little game all this time—letting you 'find' important papers I brought home, giving you access to just enough emerging intel to make your superiors believe you were an invaluable asset that helped America to win the Cold War. I let you believe these things—all while feeding you *dezinformatsiya*, disinformation we wished the U.S. to act upon—as they have."

She needed no imagination for what would follow such a conversation. Linnéa's breath caught in her throat. *I have waited too long already; it must be today!*

But what if her superiors did not approve her request? Slipping away from both Zakhar and Alyona in St. Petersburg—without assistance, without others running interference to aid her—would not prove easy. On her own, she might fail . . . and then?

Then Petroff would realize that her adoration was and always had been a sham.

Linnéa experienced a sudden, frightening insight: how close Lake Komsomolskoye was to Lake Ladoga, the largest freshwater lake in Europe—one hundred thirty-six miles long, nearly eighty-six miles wide, *seven hundred fifty-five feet deep* at its lowest point.

How many weighted bodies lined the icy depths of the lake?

She could not stop the shiver that rippled over her.

"Are you cold, my sweet?"

Think!

"No, Vassi, but I have just now sensed . . . something. An encroaching evil."

"What!"

Petroff, for all his sophistication and scientific acumen was, like many Russians, incredibly superstitious. On rare occasions, Linnéa affected to have received premonitions—forewarnings that Petroff heeded more seriously than she had believed possible. Caught now, having allowed her dark thoughts to surface, Linnéa used this ruse to distract him.

"Only an impression, Vassi, although it disturbs me."

"What is it? You must tell me!"

"*Da, da.* It was . . ." Think! *Think!*

"It-it was about the train . . . your train! Oh, I am suddenly frightened, Vassi! Perhaps you should . . . take a later train, not the morning one."

"*Zakhar!* Zakhar, come quickly!"

Petroff's roar deafened Linnéa. She withdrew from his embrace and Petroff, distracted by her presentiment, released her.

"I am here, Vassili Aleksandrovich."

"I will take the automobile to Moscow, not the train—even though the journey will take a little more time. Tell the driver to ready himself."

Zakhar slid his eyes toward Linnéa. "And Miss Olander?"

"You will call for a rental car and escort her to her office in St. Petersburg; take Stepan to drive for you. Also, Alyona will accompany Miss Olander as usual," Petroff commanded.

Linnéa swore in silence. She had, through painstaking machinations, acquired her own key to Petroff's car: If Marstead's decision were to go against her in St. Petersburg, she was prepared to appropriate Petroff's luxurious automobile—to elude Zakhar, if ever-so-briefly—in order to give herself a head start.

A rental car quashed that hope.

Linnéa berated herself for her mistake. *Stupid, stupid, stupid!* If Marstead would not help her, she would be forced to access more "creative" methods of escape.

Petroff turned to Linnéa. "You will not mind that I take the car? The rental will be suitable?"

Maintaining a docile, compliant countenance, she replied, "Mind? Not at all, Vassi. Naturally, you must take the car; I wish you to be safe."

He preened under her care and concern. "I will leave sooner than planned, then." Petroff left their room, shouting for his driver and valet.

Before Alyona returned to interfere, Linnéa opened her Bottega Veneta handbag and poured its contents out onto the bed. Marstead had altered the roomy purse for her needs. Linnéa had designed the customizations herself.

Her fingers found a small tab in the seam of the purse's bottom lining. She tugged. With a soft "snick," the inside layer of the purse's flat underside came free.

From beneath her pillow, she withdrew a thin case containing two CD-ROM disks. She placed the case flat on the purse's bottom and fit the loose inner layer over it. She pressed it until it locked in place with an imperceptible click. Gathering her purse's contents, Linnéa dumped them back into her purse.

With her plans in place, she closed her suitcase, zipped it, and unbent.

Either today or tomorrow, I will break free . . . or I will die trying.

End of Preview

Purchase ***Laynie Portland, Retired Spy***
in print or eBook format
from your preferred online book retailer!

About the Author

Vikki Kestell's passion for people and their stories is evident in her readers' affection for her characters and unusual plotlines. Two often-repeated sentiments are, "I feel like I know these people," and, "I'm right there, in the book, experiencing what the characters experience."

Vikki holds a Ph.D. in Organizational Learning and Instructional Technologies. She left a career of twenty-plus years in government, academia, and corporate life to pursue writing full time. "Writing is the best job ever," she admits, "and the most demanding."

Also an accomplished speaker and teacher, Vikki and her husband Conrad Smith make their home in Albuquerque, New Mexico.

To keep abreast of new book releases, sign up for Vikki's newsletter on her website, **http://www.vikkikestell.com**, find her on Facebook at **http://www.facebook.com/TheWritingOfVikkiKestell**, or follow her on BookBub, **https://www.bookbub.com/authors/vikki-kestell**.

www.faith-filledfiction.com | www.vikkikestell.com

Made in the USA
Columbia, SC
03 August 2021

42903759R00111